PROPHET STREET POET

Derrick Jones

PROPHET STREET POET

Dedication

I dedicate this masterpiece to the "Watchers."
To my mother, words can't describe…
Just know you're always on my mind…
To my big brother, Wilbert Clark, the "Humble
Hero." This one's for you, for us, and for the
dynasty, we're destined to build...
Oh, yeah, to that "Butterfly Gemini"
You know what it is….

To be continued.

Table on Contents

THE HISTORY 2022

It was a clear black night, a clear white moon, I was walking out of my spot while on the phone with my "Boo".

"You better be on your way Nation."
"Listen Tiara, I'm walking towards the car, as we speak..I see you got an APB out on me because I just got a text from Harmony saying that she's down the street and on her way!

Tiara laughed, then shot back "Well you know that girl thinks she's your bodyguard!!"

While walking towards the parking lot, some dude wearing a hoodie approached me and asked, "Ain't you that nigga that rap named Nation?"

I replied nonchalantly, "Yeah that's me, what's up, what's the word?" I turned to push the alarm to unlock the car. Out of nowhere, with a familiar voice the dude uttered "Yo, pussy, you're no blood clot prophet." In one swift simultaneous motion, I grabbed my burner off my hip and raised it. But as I was raising, he was blazing! He hit me three times before I was able to let off a couple of shots. Mortally wounded, I was on the ground leaning against my car. Just as I was fading out of consciousness he shot me again. I was done. But my assailant didn't get a chance to flee. My lioness, Harmony ran up from behind and let him have it, emptying the clip in a fit of rage.

I bet you think this is one of those shoot'em up bang-bang drug deal gone bad stories. Even though it does have some of those elements within it, it's far more in-depth than that.

This story began a half-millennia ago in Africa, with a King named Aswad. Aswad was a righteous pure-hearted King of Aswanna. Since a fledgling, he had been a devoted member of the ancient mystical order of "Apex Omega." One night, Aswad was visited by the first great "Supreme Steward" of Aswanni ancestry in spiritual form. His ancestor imparted the spirit of Rhythm Mystic Poetry within Aswad, then ordered him to use this spiritual gift to unite all the tribes of Africa.

While Aswad was on a diplomatic tour, his second in command, Kwannzia went behind Aswad's back and made a deal with foreigners. So when Aswad came back from the first wave of what was to be many tours, he was assassinated by Kwannzia who in turn took the throne. But while on the throne, he too was assassinated by those foreigners. They then enslaved the inhabitants of Aswanna and dispersed them across the globe. Throughout their descendants' time in America, there had always been a myth or a legend, that a descendent from Aswad's tribe would rise again, to reclaim the throne and fulfill the prophecy of uniting Africa.

A pure heart is born (I) Sept 13, 1996

September 13th, 1996, I came rushing out of my mother's womb with all ten fingers and toes, a head full of hair and what seems to be a birthmark of an ancient Omega symbol, on the lower right side of my neck. It was later known that I was born on the night of that day Tupac Shakur passed away. My father was also gunned down that same night in a drug deal gone bad. A tropical storm hit Houston that night, which flooded the streets and knocked out all the power in the area. So when my mother's water broke, she was stranded in the house because my father was gone in the car. Thank the ancestors, my aunt Fran was there to help deliver me.

"Push, girl!! Push!!"
Ahhh!!! Where in the hell is Fred!!!??
"Okay, breathe! Now push -- I can see his head girl, push!!"
AHHHH!!

After my father was killed, my old man's father, Grandpa Boo-Bee took it upon himself to be the father figure in my life. I was told that Boo-Bee fell in love with me the first time he saw me.

"Yep, he's from my clan, same big head and lips!!"

He would come to get me from my mother's on the weekend to show off to the ladies he called "Shoppers." Boo-Bee was an old player who had his hands in all kinds of schemes that required him to be at his "headquarters." His headquarters was a hole-in-a-wall juke joint where he was the head of a band named after him called Boo-Bees Blues Band. I would be in there toddling around while people smoked, drank and gambled, along with everything else you could imagine. I still have a picture of Boo-Bee holding me on stage. Rumor has it, that night after performing, Boo-Bee grabbed me from one of his females, raised me in the air and proclaimed, "This is my grandson, he's going to be one of the greatest musicians of all time!"

Boo-Bee was a ladies man, but this particular woman named Gwen was his Achilles heel. She was a beautiful, light-skinned Creole with gray eyes. My mother told me she had Boo-Bee wrapped around her finger. She would play mind games with Boo-Bee which somehow made him physically sick. Word on the street was she knew voodoo and had cast a spell on him; which leads me to tell you about the first assassination attempt on my life.

As the story goes, I was at Boo-Bee's for the weekend. One Saturday, Boo-Bee had to go to his juke joint early to handle a few things to prepare for that night's festivities. He had left me with Gwen not knowing she had sinister plans in the making. When

Boo-Bee left, she grabbed a suitcase, packed her belongings and placed them next to the front door. She grabbed me from the baby's crib where I slept. Next, she took me to the den where she set up an altar to perform a ritual. She laid me down on a cloth on the table while chanting in some unknown tongue. Afterwards, she smeared blood on my forehead from a bowl. In her left hand, she grabbed a chicken's foot and started waving it around while lighting incense which fogged the room up.

While she prepared to sacrifice me, Boo-Bee was on his way to the juke joint when it dawned on him that he left the money stashed in his closet; he needed money for a move he was planning so he turned around. When he finally made it back home and unlocked the door, I was told I screamed out an eerie cry which shook him to the core. He told my mother when he walked into the house he heard chanting and smelled smoke from incense burning. It all seemed unreal to him. He followed the trail of smoke to the den, where he saw her standing over me with a knife in her hand.

Seeing that he yelled, "Gwen what the hell are you doing?!"

She turned around, screamed at the top of her lungs, and in a fit of rage charged Boo-Bee with the knife. He sidestepped her, then dropped her with a punch to the face. He snatched me up, ran to the living room, and called the police.

When the police finally arrived they took Gwen into custody. Boo-Bee stood stunned while holding me as they put her in the back of the police car. "Gwen," he pleaded, "I don't understand, why would you want to kill my grandson?"

She screamed psychotically, "I wanted the honor of destroying prophecy!"

Boo-Bee stood mystified.

First Encounter (2)

Boo-Bee ended up becoming my full-time parent due to my mother's drug addiction. So for 10, 11 years I lived with him. It was a pretty peaceful laid-back life, shit I didn't want for nothing. It's times I think back, about how oblivious I was to the shit he had going on around me. I realize how he tried to conceal that underworld element from me. Boo-Bee was a musician so naturally he would bring home different forms of music like Jazz, Rock, Reggae, Afro-beat, Country, and Hip-Hop. He had mixed feelings about Hip Hop. He'd say stuff like,

"Back then hip hop had a message, now it's just a mess!"

But he couldn't block that gravitational pull that hip-hop had on this 9, 10-year-old. So he brought me Hip Hop albums that he thought would school me psychologically. There I was, home from school, sitting in my room, doing homework listening to dudes like Nas, Talib Kweli, K-Reno, Andre 3000, and Tupac.

Without a warning my life turned upside down. Boo-Bee drank hard liquor like fish drank water, and over time it took a toll on him. He died suddenly from cirrhosis of the liver. So I had to move back with my mother, which was a serious culture shock. In the blink of an eye, I went from one realm of the game to the next. I went from being surrounded by Boo-Bee's cohort of hustlers to living with my mother and her band of fiends. My mother's apartment was a crack house. At all times of the day dealers and smokers would be running in and out of the apartment like a 7/11. We wouldn't have electricity for months at a time. Anything that Boo-Bee had bought me that was of value came up missing. Shit was just crazy. I tried to withdraw myself from this environment. Most of the time, I would stay in my room reading and writing. Those days when the sun went down, I'd light a candle and put on my headphones to escape from all the turmoil that was going on around me. During that time, dudes like Lupe and Kanye kept my spirits up.

One night I was in my room, lying in bed looking at the ceiling when a faint golden glow appeared at the foot of the bed. I looked as the spirit of a man began to take shape. He was wearing a crown with jewels around his neck and wrist. His clothes were of ancient African royalty, which made him look majestic. I was initially stunned then spooked! I rose up, placing my back against the bed's headboard. Looking at him my fear began to subside; he seemed heartbroken. I could see the grief on his face. He never said a word although a solitary tear dropped from his eye. I watched in amazement as he waved his golden staff then disappeared. That would be the first time King Aswad appeared to me.

Puppy Love (3)

As time passed I began to venture into the neighborhood where I met Big Doe. Doe was a little older than me around fourteen. He was a fly, lil' fat nigga who ran routes throughout the hood for the older Dope boys. We used to hang outside the apartments' gate and watch out, while the D-Boys rat raced to cars

17

trying to hit licks. That's where I met the girl of my dreams. It was puppy love at first sight.

Her name was Tiara. She and her older cousin Peaches were coming across the street from the store. Doe knew Peaches, so he spoke to her as she walked from the store.

"Hey, Peaches, what you got in the bag?"
Peaches playfully answered, "None of yo bizznezz."
Doe lightheartedly reached for her bag, pleading for what was in there.
"Damn, boy! Here," she said while handing him the bag.

I was gawking at Tiara when Doe embarrassed me while pulling gummy bears out of her bag.

"Hey, Peaches! My lil' partner ain't took his eyes off your cousin yet!
Put him on!" Peaches laughed as my face flushed.
Peaches responded, "He is kind of cute."

Tiara trailed, bobbing her head to whatever music she was listening to in her headphones. Peaches tapped her on her shoulder to get her attention.

"Hey, that boy wants to talk to you."

Tiara approached my nervous ass and asked my name.

I mustered up the nerve and answered, "My name's Nation."

"That's a pretty name. My name is Tiara, but people call me Asia. Do you stay around here?"

I didn't want her to know where I lived because my house was the neighborhood crack house, so I lied.

"No, I'm just here for the summer."

"Oh, I'm not from here either, I'm from Baltimore. I'm just here for the summer too."

Doe noticed me fumbling so he saved me by saying, "Nation let's go get something to eat. I'm hungrier than a hostage!"

Breathing a sigh of relief I said,"I guess I'll see you around" as we walked off.

And that I did. We hung out the whole summer together. We went to a lot of places, or should I say she took me to a lot of places because I didn't have any money, shit I was broke. She came from a family that had some money. Her mother was a doctor and her father owned his own business so they ensured she was straight. We would catch the Metro everywhere: to the mall, skating rinks, movies, and any other place pre-teens went to escape their boredom. The highlight of that summer was when she took me while being chaperoned by Peaches to see Drake, Chris Brown, and Bun B in concert at the Woodlands Pavilion. That was my first time at a hip-hop concert, and that shit was super lit!

Tiara would call me every morning so we could meet up. She was staying with Peaches and her aunt in the same apartments I lived in. But I was so embarrassed by the fact that I lived in a crack house, I would tell her to meet me down the street. One night, I was in front of the apartment arguing with my mother over those crackheads keeping me up at night when Tiara and Peaches walked past. I was so embarrassed although Tiara never asked or said anything about it.

The summer was ending and the school year was about a week away. Tiara and I were hanging out on the block, sitting on one of those box generators. We watched as the D-boys did their thing while the sun set on the corner. Somebody pulled up on the block in a candy-red Cts on swangas jamming Lil KeKe's "In These Streets." We were both nodding our heads to the music when she asked,

"Nation, what do you want to be when you grow up?"

I thought about it for a second as I continued to bob my head. I hopped off the generator and in the flyest MC stance I could muster proclaimed, "A rapper!!"

She laughed and shot back, "Boy you can't rap!"

Just as I was about to spit some bars, someone yelled "Laws!" I grabbed Tiara's hand and we took off running. Although I wasn't pumping, I didn't want to be around once the laws swoop down on the block. Everybody was a suspect and subject to go to jail. About an hour passed before we decided to return to where we were sitting. And that's when she hit me with the news I knew would eventually come.
"Nation."

"Hey."

"You know school starts next week and my parents want me to leave in the morning to prepare."

Even if I wanted to respond I didn't know what to say so I said nothing. She grabbed my hand as we both sat silently for a few moments. The realization of that being our last night hanging out together had set in.

She rose up from the generator, kissed me on the cheek then said, "You have my number, don't forget to call me," and walked away. I sat silently, gazing at the moon, feeling like all the blood had drained out my little heart.

Plugged In (4)

It was the first day of school and my first day at Hastings High. I walked into the lunch room to eat and heard music being played. Like a moth to a flame, I was pulled towards the music's direction. There was a circle of dudes free-styling around the radio that was playing instrumentals. The beat switched ever so often, along with who rapped. As I positioned myself closer to listen, the instrumental of Lil' KeKe's and Big Hawk's "Superstars" came on. It felt as though an electric current flowed through my body which propelled me to flow.

"Land of the free and home of the brave,
I'm the offspring
From a descendent of slaves,
I was born in the slums of the USA,
The United States trying to find my place,
Hey, I was born in the slums and cracks,
I was born to spit hard about,
the slums and cracks,
In a trap house late night,
Preparing the crack,
With a Pyrex, microwave,
Bringing it back, Yep!
Get rich or die trying,
Like 50 Cent said, got damn, I'm trying
From a child to juvenile,
Young and defiant,

I'm a hot-headed young nigga,
Spitting that fire!!"

I spit a few more bars and once I was done, the lunch room went bananas! I started getting high-fives, daps, and hugs from everyone as the bell rang for the next period. As we dispersed to our assigned classes one of the dudes who was also in the freestyle session approached and embraced me.

"Hey, man you're nice with the flow – What do you go by?"
"Nation."
"They call me Jay. Where you from, my nigga?
I'm from the North Side, Wayside and Tidwell."
Jay asked, "Have you ever been in a studio?"

Little did we know how that day would play a pivotal role in the fulfillment of prophecy.

Unexpected (5)

That Saturday, I was at Rod-D's Studio with Jay dropping my vocals for the first time. Jay was around fifteen at that time, a few years older than me. But the nigga was light years ahead of me when it came to getting money, macking bunnies, and seeing through dummies. We hung out together on the regular. Dude taught me how to cook work, the latest swag, and how to approach females. In return, I taught him how to write music. He thought it was even trade because he felt I was the best he'd ever heard. I looked up to Jay. In my mind, this nigga had it all together. He was like a big brother to me.

Most days after school, we would go to his apartment. We'd try to be in and out before his "T-Lady'" meaning mother got home from work. He had a makeshift studio in his room where he'd try to make beats, using Pro Tools or Fruity Loops. He would be in the kitchen cooking up work; I would be in the room writing verses. Jay would be like, "Nation, let me hear something." I'd go to the kitchen and he'd have two Pyrexs going in and out of the microwave simultaneously. I'd spit the verses while he nodded his head and cooked up circles.

We rehearsed regularly because of a school talent show we had coming up. We went to Rod-D's studio and dropped what became a neighborhood hit called, "Rite of Passage." We performed it at the talent show. We didn't win, but we rocked that muthafucka! One night, we went to his uncle's spot, which was also his plug. When we got to the living room, we both took a seat on the couch. His uncle along with a few other hustlers were in the kitchen cooking up work. Unc finally came out of the kitchen. He had a pyrex in his hand surveying the contents of the jar.

"Lil' Jay, what's up, nephew? Who that you got with you?"

Jay answered, "This my lil homie I rap with, the one that was on that song, I let you hear a while back."

"Oh, yeah! You Nation?" He asked while walking back to the kitchen.

Unc continued, "Yeah, Lil' Nation, you got something, you're nice with it for real. Jay, what's up? Talk to me, what do you need?"

"Unc, I need a 1-2-5, but I'm a lil short."

"A lil short? How short, nephew?"

"Bout four hundred dollars."

Unc and everyone in the kitchen burst out laughing! "Damn nephew, you already three hundred dollars in the hole. You think I do this shit for fun or something? I know why your ass short because of you tricking off your bread at Onyx! I heard about you lil nigga, the streets be watching!"

Everyone continued laughing. Dude was funny as fuck, he had my stomach hurting! "Naw Unc, it ain't like that! I've been putting my money into this mixtape me and Nation working on and it's costing a lil more money than I thought! Work with me Unc, you know I got you shit, I'm your nephew!"

"Yea, whatever nigga! How you gone have me and them hoes at the same time! How that shit work!"

While they kept talking, I asked where the restroom was and he pointed in the direction of it. In the restroom, I unbuckled my belt, and just as I was about to pull my man out to piss; I heard a loud BOOM!! Then a succession of rapid gunshots rang out. I pulled my pants up as fast as I could, went to the window, hopped out of it, and caught the ghost.

When I got back home, I tried contacting Jay but got no answer. Later that night, I happened to watch the news and there it was "HOME INVASION!!"

Everyone in the spot was dead! Those next few days, my mind was fucked up I was paranoid as fuck. I stayed home from school, and sat in my room schvitzing, not knowing what to do next. About a week later, one morning, I was in bed asleep when the police kicked the door in and took everyone to jail. I thought it was about what happened to Jay. Come to find out, the law had a warrant for my mother's arrest. She went to jail and I ended up in a foster home.

Run Away (6)

I didn't stay at the foster home for long at all. As soon as I got a chance, I took everything I had of value and vanished. Before I knew it, I was back on the Southwest side. During the day I tried to hock the bullshit I clipped from the foster home for money to buy food. At night I'd sleep at the bus stop on Bissonnet by Woodfair. Every night for a week, around the same time, a

black Benz would pull up at the light, playing Reggae music. One night, the passenger rolled down the window.

"Ay, youth you not have nowhere to stay?" He spoke with such a thick Jamaican accent I couldn't understand him.

"What?" I responded, confused.
The woman driving translated for him.
"He wants to know if you have a place to stay?"
I tentatively answered, "Yeah, I do."
She asked, "Are you hungry?"

That caught a fat boy's attention but I didn't reply. As soon as the light turned green, she offered, "If you're hungry, get in and we'll get you something to eat."

Now to all the kids reading this; don't try this at home. The two reasons I decided to go with them were one, I was starving, and two, because of the beautiful female that was driving. So, I grabbed my belongings and hopped in the back seat.

My Savages (7)

About thirty minutes later, we arrived at our destination in Sugar Land, Texas. The house we pulled up to had nothing but Benzes, BMWs, Lambos, and other foreigns in and around the driveway. The house was two stories with a four-car garage. When I got out of the car, it was a festive atmosphere with Reggae music blasting from the balcony. There was a crowd of people drinking, smoking and dancing.

I followed them into the house and saw more of the same. I thought I was at a club!! The Jamaican dude directed me to the couch. I took a seat and continued to watch the scene. About ten minutes later, the woman came out of the kitchen with a plate of curry chicken, "rice and peas," along with a cup of juice. As I began to eat, she told me that I could go upstairs once I was done eating.

I finished the food, grabbed my stuff, and went up to the bedroom. I surveyed the room, then noticed the bathroom, and sighed with relief. It had been days since I'd taken a shower. I got my clothes out of my bag and went to shower. Once I got myself together, I got in bed and went to sleep.

The next morning, I was awoken by the beautiful woman named Renae. She had brought some breakfast from Waffle House. When I went downstairs, the Jamaican dude named Savage was puffing on a fat spliff, while surfing channels on the plasma T.V.

As he passed the spliff to Renae, he spoke.

"Yo, youth, mi a take you to get something for wear." I still couldn't understand him. Renae saw my confusion and again translated what he said.

Then she asked, "What's your name?"

"My name's Nation."

"Well, Nation, in due time you'll understand what he's saying."

As time passed, I began to make out what he was saying. Shit, I was with him every day. I rode along with him when he made moves. He would be all over Houston, dropping off, picking up, and meeting people at various places. Once I started piecing together what they were saying, I realized that these niggas were who they called "Bad-Men!" I should have known that earlier by the guns and bullet wounds they had on their bodies. They were known in the streets as the "Fifty Caliber Crew." I was surrounded by an infamous gang of Jamaican niggas, and didn't even know it! And Savage was the eye of the pyramid. Most of the time, we'd meet at one of the many shops they owned. Before we'd go out, especially on the weekend, the whole team would meet at one of their spots. Out of the twenty or so, yardmen in the crew, the ones I was most familiar with were Block Boy, who was the oldest and loudest of the crew; Doggy, the player, Shawn, and Rock the brothers, Young Soldier, and my boy Monk, who was half-Colombian, half Jamaican, all killer.

New Year (8)

The whole crew fell into Club Riddims on New Year's night. I was amped up because this was my first time in any club. The DJ was jamming a mix of Hip Hop, Reggae, and Afro-beat music. I made a B-line over to the DJ booth then got the DJ's attention: He had known I could spit from past sessions we had, when he DJ'd at Savage's home but this was a way larger crowd.

"Yo, Nation! Happy New Year!
"Ay, Digital, what's up, big bro?! I see you rocking the crowd! Put me on and let me rock this mutha fucka with you!"
"Yo, my youth, you think you can handle it!?"
"Hell Yeah!"

"Alright youth, hold on." He pushed a few buttons on the beat machine, then passed the headphones to me so I could hear the instrumental. It was that Nikki and Drake song "Moment for Life." He saw my approval of the track by the way my eyes lit up. He switched a button on the machine so that the crowd could hear, gave me a mic and started MC'-ing.

"Yo, mi got my youth Nation, from the fifty Cal Crew in here New Year's night, bout to rock the mic!!" get-'em my youth!"
I then turned up.

"Microphone check, 1-2, 1-2!"
I'm the youngest of the crew, of you know who,
A diamond in the rough, a rose sprout up,
in this concrete jungle, my nigga, I'm too tough,

I can do this all night, ya hear me, rock the mic,
All I need is a shot of vodka on ice,
The women in this club, they looking real nice,
The girl, standing next to Monk, is my type!..."

The crowd was vibing, bobbing their heads to the music. I noticed how Savage and Renae looked at each other then at me, while smiling. I continued for a few minutes then finished my session. The crowd loved me. Everybody wanted to know who I was. The girl I rhymed about next to Monk actually tried to get at me! Shit, I had just turned fifteen, I wasn't even supposed to be in the club!

Vibing (9)

A week or so later, I was at the studio that Renae had plugged me in. Renae was like, "Boy, you created a buzz quickly. Digital made a mixtape with you on it and the streets want to hear more!" So there I was, in the booth dropping' "sixteens." When I came out of the booth, the producer named Moe handed me the smoke. He played the track so that we could hear it out loud.

We were both vibing to the track when my stomach started growling.

"Hey Moe, is there something to eat in this mutha fucka?"

Moe answered, "Nah man, you might have to go up the street to the corner store." He pulled a few dollars out and handed them to me.

"And bring back some blunts too."

I grabbed my windbreaker off the hanger and walked out of the door. The convenience store was just up the street so I decided to walk. While walking, I tried to fire up the rest of the blunt I had left, but the wind kept blowing the lighter's flames. I tried once more and finally got it lit. Suddenly, I was stunned by the spirit of King Aswad in my path.

The first thing I said was, "Damn, you can't keep popping up on me like that!! You scared the shit out of me!" I had been used to his presence by then because he'd been appearing to me periodically speaking, other times observing. I returned to walking and resumed the conversation.

"So your Highness to what do I have the honor of being in your presence?"

"My son, there's great power within you. You have the power to awaken a slumbering giant."

Being young, I couldn't comprehend what he was saying. He continued,

"Your people await your arrival but you have much to learn."

As I approached the corner store, I flicked the doobie on the ground.

"Yeah, I hear you king.

Introduction (10)

Digital continued to feature me in his mixes. Over time my buzz grew larger. I was becoming somewhat of an underground name. I was opening up for artists, doing promotional shows, and featuring on other artists' mixes but I wasn't seeing no money. One afternoon I was hanging out at the mechanic shop with

Savage and the crew steaming. Savage got a call and was a little upset. I'd overheard what was said, so after the call I asked, "What's good Savage? Everything straight?" He answered by sucking his teeth then puffing on the blunt. So I continued, "Why have a team, If you don't use your players?" He understood my metaphor and replied, "My youth, mi got mad love for you, mi not want you, all wrapped up in this business."

"Look, Savage, don't get me wrong, I appreciate everything you and Renae have done for me. Taking me in, plugging me into studios and all that but I'm not that same young dude you took in three years ago. Shit, I'm hungry, I need some bread. Put me on a play so I can eat!"

Savage hit his spliff and meditated on what I had said for a moment.

"Nation, you think you're ready, huh?"
"Hell yeah, I'm ready."
"Alright, my youth, mi have a play for you."

Harmony (11)

The next thing I knew, I was landing in Hartsfield - Jackson airport in Atlanta with 200 pounds of "loud." Montana Ranks pulled up in the terminal in a Range Rover. He hopped out and raced to help me put the luggage in the back of the Range.

"Nation, my youth! wagwan!? Long time no see!"
"What's up with it Ranks! It has been a few years right!"

I had met Ranks a few years back in H-Town at one of the crews' hang-out spots. He and Monk got into a shoot-out with some niggas in Fif-Ward. He walked with a limp, after being shot a few times in the ordeal. We hopped in the Range Rover and took off. There were two beautiful women in the truck, one riding shotgun with Montana, whose name was Maxine. The other was in the back seat, Harmony. Harmony was a drop-dead gorgeous, caramel-complected island girl. She looked like an Egyptian goddess. We greeted each other as Montana introduced me to them.

"Hey gals, this Nation, my youth from H-Town. Them his tunes I've been jamming."

Harmony enthusiastically responded, "Oh, damn you sound really good!"

"I appreciate that lady."

I had to turn my head before I got lost in her eyes. Montana turned up the music which was playing one of my songs from Digital's mixtape. We arrived at Montana's home and pulled into the driveway. When we all got out, the ladies went inside, while Montana helped me with the luggage. Once in the house, I put the luggage with my clothes in the room. The luggage with the work went to the kitchen.

I went back into the living room and sat on the couch. Harmony came out of the den and as she walked toward the kitchen asked,"Do you want something to drink?"

I, thinking she wasn't going to bring it, answered playfully, "Yeah, vodka on the rocks, no chaser." A moment later, she came back with two glasses in her hand then took a seat next to me. She handed me a glass, reached for the blunt in the ashtray, and fired it up.

"So, Nation, how long have you been rapping?"

"Whew, on and off all my life."

"You sound really good. You have a lot of style and charisma."

I modestly replied, "Thanks."

While we were talking, someone came out of the backroom and walked toward the kitchen. We acknowledged each other by nodding our heads at one another, as he walked into the kitchen. Harmony carried on quizzing me,

"Nation, how old are you? You look like a baby."

"I'm seventeen."

"Seventeen!"

"Hey, I'll be 18 in a few months!" We both laughed.

"Oh, that's why you were surprised when I brought you that drink!"

She playfully reached for the drink in my hand. I weaved her hand and took another sip. Montana came out of the kitchen and handed me a thick stack of cash.

I looked at it, shoved it in my pocket, and continued our conversation.

"Oh," I continued mockingly,

"I guess you're one of those setup gals huh!"

She pulled out a stupid-sized desert eagle from her purse.

"No, Mi do more than just set up a food. Mi eats too!!"

"Well damn!" I said mockingly as I raised my hand in surrender.

She laughed, "Boy, stop playing! I like you -- you're cute and funny."

So I asked, "How old are you?"

She put a scowl on her face and responded playfully, "You ever heard, you shouldn't ask a woman how old they are?"

"Oh, damn my fault lady, I was just making conversation."

"Boy, I'm twenty-two."

"Oh, well shit, we're practically the same age!"

Dude who'd just passed by walked out of the kitchen and looked at Harmony and then me with a tinge of animosity as he walked to the backroom. Once he'd left the room, I asked, "Who's that dude?"

"Oh, that's Rebel. That's Montana's worker."

"Shit, by the way, he looked at me just now, it's got to be more to it than that."

"And he's my ex."

"I knew it." I countered while smirking.

"Don't worry bout him, he's old news."

"Oh, that's the last thing I'm worried about."

We talked until around three that morning. She checked her cell and asked,

"How long are you staying in Atlanta?"

"It depends."

"Depends on what, "likkle boy?"

"Depends on how things look out here."

"O.K. smart ass." She got up to leave.

On the way toward the door she carried on, "I'm gonna come link up with you in the morning and take you around Atlanta."

When she reached the door; she continued, "Come lock the door silly."

I got up to lock the door. Once I reached the door to lock it, we stood face to face, and she kissed me. Afterward, she walked out and left. I locked the door and turned around, this nigga Rebel was lurking by his bedroom door.

A.T.L (12)

Around eleven that morning, I was awakened by a text from Harmony, saying that she was on her way. I went to the bathroom and got fresh. Afterwards, I took out about two grand from the "bag" that Montana had given me for transporting that work. I laid back in bed until I received a text from Harmony saying she was outside. At the same time, Montana knocked on the door and as I approached it, he opened it.

"My youth, what's up?"

"I'm good."

"Yo," He revealed while smiling, "The gal outside in the car is waiting for you."

As I walked out of the room, towards the living room, I answered "Thanks for letting me know." I opened the door to go outside. Harmony was sitting in a phat champagne-colored BMW 760i on Giovanna rims. I got in while she rolled down her window to speak to Montana. Rebel was in the garage, looking like a square. You could see the malice on his face, as Harmony backed out of the driveway to leave.

The first place she took me was to get something to eat at this Caribbean restaurant called Bahama Breeze. I followed behind as she led the way in. I noticed how that Louis Vuitton skirt she wore fit the contours of her curvaceous body. I had to secretly catch my breath. I thought to myself, "Damn she's drop-dead gorgeous."

We sat down at the table. I ordered some beef and rice; she ordered a plate full of vegetables. As we began to eat, I looked over at her plate.

"Hey, you don't have any meat on your plate.
What's up with that?"

She shot back, "I'm a vegetarian."

"A what?" I said "poking" at her, "You got to be
bullshitting me!"

"I've never seen one of those kinds of people in real
life!"

She let out a good laugh.

"So Nation, where do you want to go today?"

I thought for a second, then answered, "I want to
check the Civil Rights Museum."

She pulled out her cell phone from her purse, then
googled the address.

"It's not far from here."

Walking through the halls of the Civil Rights
Museum, observing the portraits, pictures, and exhibits
weighed heavily on my soul. I stood in front of the
photo of Emmett Till and thought of what just recently
happened to Trayvon Martin.

I uttered somberly, "Damn, that could've been
me."

Harmony sensed the sorrow that developed within me; she put her hand on my shoulder to comfort me without saying a word. We walked to where there was a remake of a Slave ship exhibit. While we were observing the conditions our ancestors had to endure on those slave ships, I spotted King Aswad watching me from the corner of the exhibit.

We ventured to a Black Panther exhibit admiring all the leaders, and fallen soldiers who had died fighting for freedom, equity and equality. The whole experience was serious. We left the museum, got in her BMW and shot off. While she was driving her phone rang.

"Yo, Dre-Bo what's up? Yeah, ok we'll link up soon." She finished the call and hung the phone up.

"Nation, baby, mi link some studio time for you."
I playfully shot back, "How do you know I feel like rapping?"
"Aw, baby don't do that. Mi want my mix of you that's all."

"Alright lady, just because it's you. And the way you switch your voice from Yankee to Yardee just does something to me!"

We pulled into Buckhead. She drove to the gate, made a call and the gate opened. We drove in and parked along the cul-de-sac. When we got out, a beautiful woman was standing in the doorway waiting for us. We greeted her, then followed her to the back where the studio was located. There was a small crowd hanging out around the studio. They were all rocking Atlanta Falcons red and black bandanas in their pockets and necks. There was also someone in one of the two booths spitting bars.

I took a seat. Harmony went to speak to the person working on the mixing board. He took his headphones off, raised from his chair, and embraced her.
    "Hey, Dre-Bo baby... How are you?
    "I'm good, lady. How bout yourself?"
    "I'm fine." She gestured towards me and continued,
    "That's Nation, the one I was telling you about."

Dre-Bo approached me, as I got up to greet him. We shook hands.

"What's up, Nation, you ready?"

"Yeah, just bring me a shot of vodka."

The dude in the booth came out.

"Yo, Dre let me hear how I sound on them Bose speakers!"

Dre went to the mixer and turned the track on so everyone could hear. It was a club banger, everybody was bobbing their heads in unison. A beautiful dark-skinned slim chick came back with a bottle of Grey Goose vodka and some cups, to let us pour out our troubles. The song ended and Dre-Bo gestured at me to get into one of the booths. I walked into the booth and put on the headphones. Through the headphones, I heard Dre-Bo say,

"We're just gonna do a little vibing'"

"Alright."

"Tell lil homey to come to trade a few bars with me."

Lil homie walked into the second booth and put on the headphones. Dre-Bo played the track. I was bobbing my head, but I wasn't really feeling the track. Lil homie caught the rhythm and rocked the track. Dre-Bo could tell I wasn't feeling the track so he mixed in another track, while the dude finished his verse. Lil' homie was merciless; he rocked that track as well. But I wasn't digging that track either. After Lil Homie finished that track, Dre-Bo turned the music off.

"Nation, what's up with you, man?"
"I apologize for being a lil "bougie" when it comes to tracks."
"Well, tell me what you like then."
"I like that classy sound, with a lot of piano and flutes——-that live band sound, you know what I'm saying?"
"Okay, I know just what you are looking for."

While we waited for Dre-Bo to play the next track, I asked Lil Homie his name. He called himself "Top Star." Top for short.

"Well, Top Star, you're nice with the flow, for real." Right then the next track came on. "Three times a charm!" I announced as I gave Dre-Bo two thumbs up indicating that it was the right track. Before I continue, I want to give the readers an idea of how the track sounded. It was jazzy, like Biggie's "I Love The Dough" with that Jay-Z's "As Real As It Gets"-feel to it. We let the track breathe for a minute, then I signaled at Top to go first. He did just like he had on previous tracks, which was "kill" it. He signaled for me to go. Once I caught the rhythm, I looked Harmony in her eyes then began with:

"Come on Lady,
I'm young, but I'm old school like the eighties,
They said I wouldn't make it, but damn, I made it,
you can tell, by how them rims, sitting on that
Mercedes, King!
Something like a mayor,
major, player, Half-man, half amazing,
You know life be so crazy,
 But you gotta keep it pushing, baby,
Tonight's the night, the next chapter in life,
It's like lightning strikes, Once I grab the mic..."

While I continued to spit, I noticed how the crowd reacted plus how Harmony swayed to the music.

"Through corridors of time, this is my reason to rhyme,

The reason is, I'm the next leader in line.."

I just so happened to look to the left of the crowd and noticed a silhouette of King Aswad vanishing as I finished the song. We made a few more songs, exchanged info and hung out a little bit. Dre-Bo gave us copies of the mix, then we shot off.

Rebel (13)

It was around one that morning when we arrived at this reggae bar and grill in Decatur. Harmony brought two drinks to the table from the bar.

"Here, young ass boy," she said in her yankee voice.

She laughed as she continued, "You gone get me in trouble."

I took a sip and sat it on the table. A song came on that she loved.

"Oh, that's my song! Come dance with me, Nation!"

Before I had a chance to say I didn't dance, I was pulled to the dance floor. We drew close to each other and danced in unison. While we swayed to the beat, Montana and Rebel walked in towards the bar. When Rebel saw Harmony grinding on me, he blew his top! He tapped Montana on the shoulder to get his attention and pointed to us on the dance floor.

"Yo, who the mon think him is, thinking he can touch and feel up my
gal, like so?!"

Montana replied,"Yo, that's not your gal, no more just cool, mon."

A while later, we went outside to the parking lot to get some air. I stood next to Harmony's BMW, while she sat on the hood steaming, when Rebel walked up on us. I was trying to be cordial, so I spoke. "What's up with it, rude boy?"
I tried to pass him the blunt. But this nigga Rebel replies:
Ay, pussy, go suck your mutha!"

I instinctively reached out to slap him but noticed him reaching for his burner. As he grabbed it, I snatched it out of his hand and slapped him three or four times as he fell. I stood over him when Montana and a few other yard-men ran over trying to calm the situation down.

"Yo! My youth, what happened!?"
"This bitch ass nigga, on some bull shit!"

As the yardmen helped Rebel up off the ground to take him to the car, Montana looked at Harmony.

"Oh, Now Mi know what this bout."
Harmony interjected, "Mi don't know why him so vexed, we've been done ages ago."

Montana asked, "Nation, you good?"
"Yeah, I'm cool."
"So what you going to do? Where you gonna go tonight?"
Harmony proclaimed, "He's coming with me."
"Okay, my youth, just be cool!"

Love or Lust? (14)

Harmony got a room at the Four Seasons hotel, downtown on the twelfth floor overlooking Atlanta. It had been a long and eventful day. We took turns taking showers: I took mine first, put on a robe and sat on the bed. I then turned on some music. Alicia Keys "Unthinkable" was playing when she came out of the bathroom. She had a towel wrapped around her curvaceous body. She sashayed toward the window and looked out at the view. I rose from the bed and walked over to her. When I reached her, I wrapped my arms around her waist. We both stood silently for a moment looking out at the night sky.

"This is just beautiful. This mi favorite place in the city. Mi come here when mi want to reflect on things happening in my life."

"I can see why."

The scene was serene. We stood silently again for a moment until she turned towards me and kissed me. Amid our kissing, her towel fell to the ground. I kissed and sucked down to her neck, as we motioned our way to the bed. I then took off my robe. With my hand caressing her right breast, I continued sucking on her left breast. She moaned with pleasure when I slid my right hand down to her juice box and slid my finger in. Her box was super wet.

I grabbed the condom off the dresser and put it on. She grabbed "my man" and guided him in her as she moaned with satisfaction again. We went to work on each other for about an hour and once we finished fell asleep.

The next morning Harmony woke me up and passed her phone to me.

"Yeah, what's up."
"Yo, Nation it's me, Savage. Mi heard bout what happened last night."
"Yeah, it was just a misunderstanding."
"Come home today, my youth."
"Alright, I'll soon come.."

A few minutes later, we got dressed and left the hotel. I had to stop by Montana's house to get my luggage. Although Montana assured me he'd be there and nothing would happen; when we pulled up I told Harmony to hand me her burner. Fortunately, there were no problems when I went in to get my luggage. Afterwards, she shot me to the airport.

Harmony 2.0 (15)

Harmony's sexy ass was born in Kingston, Jamaica. At the age of eleven her family packed up and migrated to Brooklyn, New York. Soon afterwards, her father flew the "coop" and left her and her mother on their own. So in order for them to survive, her mother linked up with some heavy weighters and started moving weight for them across the United States. She watched and learned from her mother how to play the game, the streets and niggas.

By the time she turned sixteen, she was well known among the yardmen circles as a beautiful, charismatic, and ambitious young temptress, who would also squeeze that iron. She was an intelligent girl with an explosive temper. She shot up her first boyfriend's spot, severely wounding two of his workers. She found out that he had "short-stopped" her bag, by going behind her back and dealing with her clientele without her.

Her mother pleaded with her stubborn ass to leave fearing that they would retaliate. She grudgingly agreed and decided to enlist in the military. She left New York and moved down south where she was stationed at Ft. Steward, GA. Four years later, after completing her tour of duty, she was discharged. She settled in Atlanta, where she'd already known Maxine, Montana, and Rebel. She and Rebel were in a relationship for a while until she broke up with him over his overbearing, possessive, and jealous ways.

Even though they had broken up, she was still associated with Maxine and Montana. They had shown her how to smoothly navigate through Atlanta's streets. Years later, she told me the night we met in the back of Montana's Range Rover, I had this faint golden glow that compelled her to gravitate to me. She was like,

"Mi knew there was something bout your likkle chubby ass!"

Lost and Found (16)

When I got back to H-Town, I fucked off all that little bread ASAP! I painted the Buick red and bought a set of swangas. After that, I was damn near broke. Besides that bullshit that happened with Rebel, the trip was a success. Savage trusted my judgment so he allowed me to make more moves. So with the little bread I had left, I put that with the work that was shooting up north too.

For about a year and a half, I tore the country up: New York, Indiana, Chi-Town, Arkansas, and Philadelphia. I was running up those frequent flier miles. While in Baltimore, I was with the crew tearing down the mall. When we came out of Neiman Marcus, I heard a female yelling my name.

"Nation!!"

I turned to the right and was surprised to see who it was. She had her arms open running towards me. She embraced me and kissed me on the cheek,

"Nation! What the hell are you doing up here!?"

I put my bags down, then stepped back to look at her. I told my partners to go on ahead, and I'll catch up with them.

"Tiara "Asia" Richards. Long time no see?" She put her hand on my chest and covered her mouth in amazement.

"Oh my God! I thought I'd never see you again!" she screamed as she playfully slapped me.
"Boy, why you never called me!?"
Ignoring her question I asked, "How have you been?"
"Fine!" she replied with emphasis.

I looked at her up and down. "I can see that." Tiara had grown to become a gorgeous milk chocolate goddess. She had a champagne glass shape with exotic features, hence her nickname Asia. She was rocking those Dolce and Gabbana tights with that turtle neck shirt.

"So, what have you been doing for yourself, lady?"
"I'm in college, majoring in communications."
"Oh yeah? That's good. I'm proud of you."
"Boy, shut up!" she said while laughing.
"So what have you been up to?"
"Ahh, just living baby."

She looked down at the bags.
"Looks like you've been living one hell of a life!"
Her phone rang. She looked at the number but ignored the call.
"Put my number in your phone, Nation. I gotta go, but you better call me."

She gave me her number, hugged then kissed me again, and sprinted off.

Re-Acquainted (17)

A few weeks later, when I touched back down in Houston, I called Tiara.

"Boy, why are you just now calling me!"

"I'm sorry baby, I had a lot of shit going on. So what's up with you?"

"Oh, I'm in traffic. I just got out of class, about to go get some Chipotle. What are you doing?'

"Just got out of the shower, about to watch Power."

"Nation?"

"What's up?"

"Why didn't you ever call me?"

I sighed for a moment, while a tinge of embarrassment echoed through me.

"Asia, do you want to know the truth?"

"Of course, I do."

"Well, first of all, it had nothing to do with you. I was in puppy love with you!"

We both laughed.

"You remember when I told you, I didn't stay on Cinnamon Lane?"

"Yeah."

"Well, I did. I was just too embarrassed to let you know because my house was a crackhouse. My mother was down bad. Around the beginning of the school year, the police kicked the door in and took everyone to jail. I went to a foster home. A short time after, my mother died in prison. I hate thinking about that time in my life because it makes me feel so vulnerable."

"Oh my God, Nation I didn't know, I'm so sorry."

"It is what it is. I'm over that. Life goes on."

"And here I Am being selfish, just thinking about myself."

"It's alright, you didn't know what was happening."

There was a solemn moment of silence. Then I resumed the conversation.

"So Tiara, where are we going to go from here?"

"Nation, I never thought I would see you again. You don't even have an instagram page! Now that you're back in my life, I don't want to let you go."

"So are we going to turn that puppy love we had into something full-grown?"

"I guess so, silly!" she responded while laughing.

Family Ties (18)

Tiara had finished the semester of that school year, so I decided to fly up there and do some cup-caking with her during the winter break. We fell with each other all over again, I felt like I did when I first met her on Cinnamon Lane all those years ago. The only thing was that in the back of my mind, there was Harmony. We hadn't spoken to each other in a while over some bullshit, but I still had some serious feelings for her.

While I was there Asia took me to her family's home, where she introduced me to her parents. Her father Mr. Joseph Richards was a Vietnam veteran who owned his own HVAC company. We sat at the dinner table conversing, while her mother Mrs. Evelyn Richards was in the kitchen preparing the meal.

"Mr. Richards, that sounds like a pretty laid-back business you are running."
"Son, It's not as easy as it sounds."
"Nation, don't let my daddy fool you--all he does is sit in his truck most of the day anyway!"

Asia joked as they both laughed.

"That's because I earned my stripes! Twenty-plus years, I built my business; Asia mockingly finished the sentence with.. "from the ground up!" I know Daddy!"

Her mother came out of the kitchen to let us know the food was ready.

She had two plates of food in her hand. She handed one to Mr. Richards and sat at the table with the other. Asia went and grabbed our plates that Mrs. Richards had made and brought them to the table.

Once we settled in to eat, we resumed our conversation.

"So, Nation," Mrs. Evelyn asked, Asia told us you two met some years back in Houston..Is that right?"

"Yes ma'am, one summer some years ago."

"Yes mama, we lost contact with each other. Then recently, I saw his butt walking out of a store in the mall! I couldn't believe it, after all these years!!

Can't be true (19)

Asia and I were playing in the bed pillow-fighting, when I received a call from Renae. When I picked up the phone to answer; she was crying.

"Renae, what's wrong?"

"They killed him, Nation...They killed him!"

"What?" I shouted, not wanting to register what she said.

"Nation, Savage is gone." When I finally accepted what was said, it seemed that my blood pressure had shot through the roof!

Asia asked, "Baby are you alright."

"I'm taking the first flight back okay, Renae."

Back in Houston, Renae picked me up from Hobby Airport and took me to Southwest Memorial Hospital to see Monk, who was in ICU. He had just recently regained consciousness. As soon as I walked to see the condition he was in, I roared like a lion: "Who in the fuck done this shit!" Monk used the remote to raise up, and weakly responded, "Rebel."

"Rebel?!" What? That bitch ass nigga? What the fuck! What the fuck happened?"

"He came down with his crew, caught us slipping, and ate our food."

"Damn! I'm gone to get this mutha-fucka."

"No, my youth, just be cool, wait till mi heal up, then we go get that pussy together.

Farewell (20)

Savage was loved and well respected. People from all over the country showed up to pay their respects. Harmony even showed up. I Hadn't seen her in over two years. When they began to lower Savage's casket to the ground, she walked over and grabbed my hand to comfort me. I whispered in her ear, "I really appreciate you being here." She then drew closer, as she gripped my hand tighter.

After the funeral, the reception was held at Renae's home. Harmony sat next to me in the backyard beneath the gazebo. The sun set and stars began to appear. I sat gazing at the stars.

"I can't believe Savage is gone. This shit can't be real."

"You ain't heard nothing bout that nigga, Rebel?"

"Yeah, mi heard him killed Montana too."

"What?! Are you serious? This nigga is out of control!"

Close to a year before, Montana had been found dead, shot in the head at a hotel. Nobody had known what happened. But as time passed, people started putting the pieces together and the streets started talking. Rebel was jealous of Montana's hand in the streets.

So, well you know how the story goes.

"He's gonna get his. That's a promise."

It took Monk months to heal. During that time, I felt as though I was losing my mind. I was spiraling out of control.

I was at my spot on the couch smoking "sherm" while sipping "drank." I grabbed the bottle of Xanax that was on the coffee table to open it when King Aswad appeared.

I growled, "What the hell are you doing here?" as I took a few pills out, threw them in my mouth and washed them down with "drank." He didn't respond so I reached for the "sherm" cigarette, fired it up and took a drag.

"Oh so, you're just gone stand there and not say nothing? I just lost the only person in the world who truly gave a fuck about me and all you can do is stand there like a fucking statue and look crazy! I don't even know why I'm tripping anyway! You don't even exist, you're just a figment of my imagination!"

I screamed as I grabbed the ashtray and threw it at King Aswad, but it went through him hitting the patio window shattering it.

Gangsta Love (21)

"Yo gal, what's up?"

"Hey babe, how are you?"

"I'm touching base with you, to let you know we're on our way there.

"You gone have them tools ready for us right?"

"Of course."

"Alright, Lady, I'll hit you when we land."

"Okay, Babe...Nation, I love you."

Damn, I thought to myself, she really do love a nigga.

The Set-Up (21)

We arrived in Atlanta around eleven that night and rented a Caravan from Avis. I phoned Harmony to let her know we were in town and to get her new address to the condo she had just moved to.

When we got there, she opened the door and jumped her sexy ass into my arms.

"Hey, baby!

She said in her yardee voice, knowing that would make me feel some type of way.

"Hey Mommy, I'm happy to see your sexy ass."

The rest of the team followed behind me into her living room. It was Monk, Shawn, Doggy, and Soldier. Harmony went into her closet, pulled out a gym bag, and sat it on the table. She unzipped it, displaying the contents of the bag.

"Here's the tools you asked for, babe."

I pulled them out and passed each tool to each person according to what they had requested.

"So, what's the word on the street, lady?"

"Word is the "mon"a run the streets red!" Rebel and crew, a mash-up everything in sight! Nobody not have nothing but him. Mi had to go to him to grab a food see."

As she carried on, we checked our tools.

"Ugh, Mi can't stand him, but mi had to deal with him."

"Okay mama, I commanded, "here's what I want you to do."

Pay Back (23)

Around two that morning, Rebel came knocking on the door with a backpack on his shoulder. Harmony had him bring a few pounds of "loud." Ole boy, you should have heard the way she wooed him. Pussy is a muthafucka; that's how Adam fell in the garden. She opened the door and he followed her into the dining room.

"Yo, gal! Rebel blurted out, as he smacked her on her ass. "You look sweet enough to eat!"

"Boy! You want something to drink?"

"Yeah, bring a Heineken, if you got any," he says while putting his backpack on the dining table.

He never saw us coming. When Harmony walked into the kitchen, I came out with my blicker drawn.

"Say, muthafucka, what's up!?"

Just as he reached for his banger, Monk came from behind and hit him across the head with his pistol. I slapped him across the face, with mines several times, as he crumbled until Monk grabbed me.

"Nah man, fuck this nigga!" I roared as tears swelled up in my eyes.

Monk shot back,"Yo, let's see where he got the money first, my youth!"

While Shawn and Soldier tied him up, Monk interrogated him.

"Where's the blood clot money? Where's the food?"

He yelled with fear, "It's in Decatur!"

Soldier and Shawn grabbed and dragged him as the rest of us followed to get in the van. Shawn took the driver's seat.

On our way to Decatur, Monk continued to torture him and demanded to know who was there.

"Who's in the house?"

Rebel didn't answer so Monk slapped him again with his banger.

Reluctantly, he fearfully answered, "Spider, Dragon, and Archie!"

"Where's the food at, pussy!?"

Not wanting to get banged upside his head again he sputtered, "In the attic, it's in the attic!"

Twenty minutes later, we parked on the side of the house. Monk taped Rebel's mouth and took the keys out of his pocket. Shawn stayed behind in the driver's seat while the rest of us hopped out guns ready. As we approached the door, Monk unlocked it. Doggy, Soldier and I rush in shooting everything in sight.

We popped the first two dudes who were sitting on the couch steaming. Someone came out of the kitchen firing and hit Soldier in the shoulder. Monk shot the dude who hit Soldier in the neck; he went down. I ran upstairs towards the attic. While all the action was going on in the house, the caravan cranked up and sped off. Doggy looked out of the blinds in a confused state and yelled, "Yo, the van a burn-off, mon!"

Monk made his way upstairs to help me with the attic. Once we got it down, I went up the stairs and yelled, "Jackpot!" I proceeded to pass all the bags filled with drugs down to Monk, who in turn "relayed" them downstairs. Doggy and Monk searched the pockets of the dudes we'd just downed for keys. Doggy found a set.

Doggy yelled, "Let's go!"

We ran to the garage. Doggy punched the alarm button to open the trunk. We threw the bags into the trunk and piled into the Benz. Once I punched the garage opener on the visor to open, we sped off and spilled into the streets.

Come to find out, this nigga Rebel had used his hunter knife stashed in his shoe, to cut through the duct tape. He snuck up on Shawn in the driver's seat then slit his throat. He pushed Shawn to the side and drove off.

We shot back to Harmony's condo. We gathered in the living room with all the bags to count it out.

Harmony patched Soldier's injury; he'd kept insisting it was only a flesh wound. Altogether there were four bricks, eleven pounds of smoke, and close to 200 hundred bands.

"Harmony, baby you may want to move cause Rebel got away."

Me not knowing at the time what happened continued, "I guess some way he got a hold of Shawn or something, cause the van drove off while we were in the house."

"Damn, mi just got this place too," she mentioned as she playfully slapped me on my chest.
"You think I'm gonna move away because of that pussy?"
"No, even though I wished your tough ass would."

We stayed a few more weeks in Atlanta to get rid of that work then flew back to Houston. After I pleaded and coaxed Harmony, she eventually moved.

Slippers Count (24)

Back in H-Town, I got a spot on Westheimer,
down the street from the Galleria. I was doing my
thang but I wasn't shooting up north like when Savage
was alive. Some niggas I met from South Park turned
me on to making moves in and around Texas. This
nigga name Polo was the "HNIC" of a clique of niggas
from Belfort. I met Polo one night at Prospect Park on
Richmond blvd. I met him through Doe's black ass,
whom I hadn't seen in years. That night we all had a
good time getting wasted while reminiscing. With Doe
vouching for Polo claiming that Polo was righteous,
over time I slowly started to rock with him. We were
getting money, strip club hopping, and hanging out
together; which led me to let my guard down around
this snake-ass nigga. You get careless around people
you're comfortable with.

One morning, Polo and a few of his boys came
over just like they did any other morning. They knock,
and I let them in, not paying attention to them. But that
morning when the pattern was repeated, these niggas
rushed in and one of them shot me in the stomach.

I fell back on my couch, yelling "Fuck!"

Polo stood over me with that banger in his hand and growled, "Nigga, you know what it is, where it's at?!"

BANG!
He shot again as the bullet pierced my shoulder.
"Ah, fuck!" I yelled.
"It's in my room closet, in my safe!"

The other two dudes rushed to the bedroom. A moment later, they came out carrying my safe in their hands.

"Where's the key at nigga?"
Clutching my stomach in agony, "Around my neck."
He snatched the key from around my neck and used it to unlock the safe.
BANG!

He shot me again in the chest, while they took everything I had in the safe. I felt myself going in and out of consciousness. Before they left, he shot me once more in the arm. As luck would have it, Renae was on her way to come get me, so we could go to Savage's gravesite together. How ironic!

When I finally, miraculously regained consciousness, Asia and Harmony were both there at the bedside in the ICU. I thought I was dreaming, but there they were hovering over me like angels.

"I'm so glad you're alive!" Asia expressed, as she continuously kissed me.

I looked over at Harmony who was just more concerned about my well-being and happy that I regained consciousness.

Renae pleaded, "Baby, you have to stop. Just give it all up. I don't want to lose you like I lost Savage. I love you. You're like my little brother."

I later learned that Renae called Tiara and Harmony and told them what happened. They flew down and once they arrived Renae introduced them to each other.

She told them about how her and Savage had found me at a bus stop and took me in.

She also told them how Savage didn't want me in the game because he had love for me, and believed in my music. Renae and Tiara continued to plead with me while Harmony stood stoned face not saying a word. I listened and promised to hang my gloves up and retire. But in my heart, I knew I wasn't finished.

It took months for me to bounce back. My lionesses were there to support me through therapy. When Asia had to leave to go back to school; Harmony would fly down to help. Over time, I got back to where I could maneuver without having to swallow a thousand pills for the pain.

The Real Triangle (25)

Tiara flew down one weekend to get her hair done by her cousin at Peaches' hair salon. On our way there, we stopped at a vegan restaurant where Harmony had a table waiting for us. We took turns embracing Harmony and took our seats across from her. I sat next to the window. Asia initiated the conversation.

"Hey, girl what's up?"

Harmony replied, "I'm okay pretty girl, how was your flight?"
"Girl, halfway here it started storming, then the plane started shaking with all that turbulence. As much as I fly, that's just something I could never get used to."

"Mi know girl tell mi bout it."

While they were talking the waiter brought us menus. After we placed our orders, we continued the conversation.

Asia asked, "Hey, I have a question for both of you."
She looked at me and Harmony, "What are we going to do about this?"

I knew what she was talking about but instead of answering I looked out the window.

Harmony's crazy ass answered," Do what bout what?"
"About this,"Asia said as she pointed her fork at me, Harmony then herself.
"Look," Harmony announced, "Mi not going no-where."
Asia countered, "Hey, I'm not going no-where either."

They both looked at me, while I looked out the window trying to avoid the conversation. Finally, I proclaimed,"Hey, I'm not going anywhere."

Asia asked, "So we're going to be polygamists then right!?"

"Yeah, like the Muslims! Harmony declared while laughing.

I tried to hide the smirk growing on my face. Asia noticed me and playfully slapped me.
"Oh, so you think you're King Joffi Joffa now!"

Sweet Revenge (26)

We pulled up outside of Peaches hair salon and sat for a moment talking.
"Nation, I wanna ask you something,"
"Okay, what's up?"
I responded as I watched people walking the sidewalk going to various places.
"Why did you tell me your mother died in prison?"
I let out a sigh, "Because she did."
"No, she didn't Nation. I know because I did some research and found her on the internet."

"Well, she's dead to me."

"Why would you say that?"

"Because I never really knew her anyway."

"Well, recently we've been corresponding with each other and I've arranged for us to go see her tomorrow."

I said nothing as I continued to look at the people walking the lot. A dude pulled in a candy-red Maserati on gorilla pokes and parked. He hopped out and got his son out of the back seat. Once he started walking with his son towards the daycare, it dawned on me who he was. It was one of them niggas who robbed me!

"Nation, do you hear me?"

"Yeah, baby I hear you."

I pulled out a stack from my pocket, peeled off like seven hundred dollars and handed it to her. When the dude came out of the daycare, I kissed Tiara.

"Look, baby, we'll go see my mother, okay? Get your hair done and call me when you're finished." She got out to go to the hair salon. I watched the dude as he got back in the Maserati and drove off. I followed two or three cars behind him. I was cautious because back then, niggas who rode red in Houston usually be on guard for niggas who wanted to "take them down" for their slabs. I followed him as he pulled into the Ludington apartments on Fondren. He punched the code to open the gate. I followed behind crawling slowly, watching as he parked by a group of niggas hanging out in the parking lot steaming.

I said to myself, "There goes that bitch Polo, right there!"

I backed up next to a dumpster and called Monk.

"Yo, Nation, waa gwaan?

"Where are you at?"

"Mi there at Cool Runnings restaurant by Club Riddims."

"Hey, I'm watching these niggas who damn near killed me over here in the Ludington Apartments."

"Enough said my youth, mi soon come."

Ten minutes later, Monk pulled into the Ludington's lot, backed in next to me, and got into my car. I hit my signal light and turned the steering wheel to the left a little bit then my stash spot opened up. I had a quarter-brick, some ski masks, and a Glock 43 in the stash. I took out the Glock, the extended clip and the ski masks. I passed one mask to Monk.

He asked with a laugh, "What's this for?"

I answered, "All them niggas didn't have anything with me getting shot."

Monk shot back, "Youth, you getting soft?"

"Nah!" I replied while laughing.

"I just don't want that much blood on my hands. Damn, I said as I paused,"I must be getting soft.

Let's go."

We pull the mask over our faces. You should have seen how them niggas reacted when we ran up on them! One of them tried to run, but Monk shot him in the lower back area. He fell to the ground in agony. There were six niggas left. I told the three, I didn't recognize to lay face down on the ground. I didn't want them niggas to see my face when I showed the niggas; who actually robbed me. I pointed the Glock at them.

"Get on your mutha fucking knees!" I demanded.

They did as they were told. I lifted my mask exposing my face.

"Yeah, Polo what's up?! Ya'll niggas remember me!? Yeah, ya'll thought y'all had me
huh!" "You bitchass niggas ain't so tough, now huh!"

All three of them niggas started crying and shit pleading for their lives! That nigga Polo, straight up pissed on himself! I raised my shirt to show my war wounds.

"You see this!? You niggas did this!"

I then did what I was there to do, which was get my revenge. I shot the other three niggas in the legs so they wouldn't attempt no-fly shit while we were fled the scene.

Dear Mama (27) "Hugging on my mama, from a jail cell"

That following Sunday morning, Tiara forced me to go see my mother at Dayton prison. She had already done seven years on a thirty-year sentence for aggravated robbery and multiple drug charges. When Tiara and I walked into the visitation room, she was sitting to the right facing the entrance door. When she saw me her eyes lit up. She waved at me to get our attention. She had aged beautifully. We walked over to her, as she rose to embrace us.

"Lord, you brought my baby to come see me!" She announced while hugging Tiara and thanking her for coming. We all took seats at the table.

"Hey, mama, you okay!?" I asked.
"I brought like twenty dollars in quarters so we can buy up a bunch of junk from the machines!"
"No baby, I'm okay, I'm just so happy to see you. You've grown up to be a handsome young man."

She turned towards Tiara and reached to hold her hand.

"I truly appreciate you reaching out to me, Tiara you're truly a godsend."

"Whew! Mama, your son is a handful."

"I can imagine. He's just like his father was."

My mother turned to me and continued, "Baby, I've missed you so much.

When I heard you ran away from the foster home I wondered whether you were dead or alive. When Tiara reached out to me and told me you were alright, my prayers were answered."

She sipped her water; then paused for a moment to think about what to say next.

"Nation, Tiara told me what happened to you."

I looked at Tiara with disgust.

"Don't look at her like that, she loves you and cares about you."

"Look mama, I'm a grown man now. I can take care of myself. Plus I don't need someone I barely know trying to tell me how to live my life."

"Nation, please! Listen." she sighed.
"Years ago, when you were a baby."

She began running down the story of the first assassination attempt on my life by Gwen. I'd heard bits and pieces of the story throughout my childhood.

She pressed on, "Initially, I didn't believe the story your grandpa Boo-Bee told me. Up until a few months ago, I always just thought he was on drugs. Tiara and I began to communicate with each other. I started praying, fasting and asking God to show me a sign. One night I received a sign, Nation. A spirit appeared to me."

When she said that, my mind flipped; I couldn't believe what I was hearing! She pressed on about King Aswad. Once it registered that she was actually talking about him, the fear of God shot through my body; I couldn't take it! Tiara looked with amazement, as I pushed from the table, and hopped up with my eyes still fixated on my mother. I back peddled towards the door.

"You know what I'm saying is true, don't you Nation! Your destiny awaits you. You are the prophet!"

My mind flipped, I didn't know what to think! I had written King Aswad off; he hadn't appeared to me since Savage's death. I thought he was just a figment of my imagination, but my mother's confirmation of his existence only made me more mentally unstable.

My Nigga Monk (28) "How long will they mourn me"

Around two in the morning one Saturday night, me and my ride-or-die Harmony were coming from 610 and West Bellfort. I had dropped off some work and picked up some bread. I drove westbound down West Bellfort, all the way towards South Gessner and decided to pull up in the Club Riddims parking lot. When I pulled into the parking lot, I heard a succession of rapid gunfire. Once I realized who it was, I immediately grabbed my burner out of the stash spot. Just as I was about to assist Monk who was firing his stick, Harmony grabbed my arm.

"Look!" she shouted as she pointed. This nigga Monk was having a Shoot out with the ATF!
"Fuck!!" I screamed.

Monk was popping up like a "jack-in-the-box" in different sections of the parking lot, weaving around cars; firing at ATF agents who were setting up a perimeter around him. All I could do was watch as they closed in on him and took the lion down, killing him on site.

Two weeks later, his family had his funeral. I didn't attend because I didn't want to see my nigga in no casket. I was psychologically shot. I went to his gravesite that night with a bottle of Jamaican Rum. I sat by his tombstone, drinking and conversing with him until the wee hours of the morning, until I dozed off. I was awakened by Tiara and Harmony who were concerned about my whereabouts. Tiara tracked my phone and found me. Harmony took my car and Tiara took me home.

Losing It (29) "Ya'll gon make me lose my mind up in here"

It was Spring Break. Peaches had just moved into the new home she had built from the ground up. She invited some of her relatives and closest friends to her housewarming party. Tiara and Peaches were in the kitchen mixing more drinks while the party resumed in the living room and game room.

"Peaches, I don't know what I'm going to do with him, girl."

"Girl, that boy's far too gone. There's only two places I see niggas like him ending up and that's either prison or the grave. I don't know why you're wasting your time, Asia. Street niggas don't last long."

"But, Peaches, I love him, girl."

While they were talking in the kitchen. I was in the game room shooting dice on the pool table. I had just sold a brick, so I had like twenty bands on me. There was this old school nigga there named C3 who was known to have lots of bread, talking shit. We all had been drinking so that just multiplied the shit-talking.

"Nigga, bet a hundred, shoot a hundred!"
"Nigga, that's punk change! Bet a thousand, shoot a thousand!"
"Fuck it, I announced, "Bet a thousand I seven in the door!"
C3 answered "Bet."

As I rolled the dice, I yelled "Hit Dice!" while I snapped my fingers, but I rolled a five.
C3 scooped up the bread and laughed.

"Boy, you gone be broke in no time!"
"Broke, Nigga Please. Bet again!" I shot two more times and lost two more grand.

Buzzing and pissed off by all of C3's high cappin'. I pulled all my bread out of my pockets and set it on the table. "This bout seventeen thousand." I then pulled out my revolver which made everyone in the room jump until I took the bullets out. "Now," I growled insanely, "Let's play a real game." I only had four bullets to start with; I put two back in the revolver. The two I had left I lobbed at C3. Out of reflex, C3 caught one out of the two, then looked at me crazy as the other fell on the table.

I spun the chamber around, put the revolver's barrel to my head and snarled, "I bet seventeen bands to your ten thousand." Then I squeezed the trigger while everyone flinched in shock. One of the females in the room ran to the kitchen.

"This nigga must got a death wish!" C3 expressed nervously.
"Is it a bet nigga?" I asked.
"Bet."

As I spun the chamber, to put the revolver to my head again the female shouted, "Asia, your man in the game room tripping!"

Asia and Peaches ran into the game room just as I was about to squeeze the trigger. When Asia saw the gun to my head she pleaded, "Nation, baby what are you doing? Please don't do this to me, baby I love you!"

She walked up to me and slowly removed the revolver from my head, took the gun and handed it to Peaches.

She hugged me, then kissed me as tears began to flow from her eyes.

"Nation, do you love me?"

"Of course I do," I answered.

"Then live. Live for me, ok?"

"Ok, mommy. But that nigga owe me ten ranks!" I proclaimed as I burst out laughing hysterically.

"I want my money!"

Truth Be Told (30)

After Spring break ended Tiara returned to Baltimore to finish the school semester. Harmony was in Atlanta at the time, but like clockwork, she flew down to be with me. Harmony and Renae had also become close friends after Savage's passing. Renae invited Harmony to move in with her. So Harmony decided to pack up her life in Atlanta, relocate and settle in Houston. A crazy thought shot through my mind. For that split second I believed she had moved to Houston just to watch over me; like some type of guardian angel but I quickly dismissed it.

Harmony was a female gangsta and knew how to handle herself in volatile situations, so I didn't mind her accompanying me as I made moves. I couldn't move like that with Tiara; she wasn't built like that, but the love and compassion that Tiara exuded was just as valuable to me. I have unconditional love for both of them. I would kill or lay down my life for both of them. They were my lionesses in that concrete American jungle.

From Way Back (31) "Hard Hit just like Haggler and Hearns"

Saturday night, I was riding with Harmony through the city. We left Prospect Park and ended up in Club Carrington's parking lot. She parked facing South Main where we could see the whole scene. The parking lot was off the chain; there were bumper to bumper slabs crawling through like a parade. She sat on the hood of her new Audi as I leaned against it, steaming. An alarm went off in our heads when we heard someone yelling my name.

We both reached for our blickers, while trying to identify where the voice was coming from. It came from a big fluffy white Benz.

"Nation! My nigga, is that you!?"

Dude hopped out of the Benz to greet me. Once I realized who it was, I had to stop Harmony from shooting him!

"I can't believe this? Jay?" I asked as he approached and we slapped fives and embraced.

"Nigga! I thought you got killed in that trap with your uncle!"

"Nah," Jay replied, "I'm here in the flesh! What's up with you?"

"You still fucking around with that rap shit?"

"Nah, man it's been a minute."

Jay reached in his pocket and pulled out a business card.

"This is my number and address to my studio, let's see if we can bring you back to life."

Walking back to the car he continued, "You were always the best I've ever heard."

The Rebirth (32)

A few weeks passed before I decided to call Jay.

"Woe, what's up with it, this Nation."

"What's up, my nigga?"

"I'm just calling to see what you got going on."

"Shit, I'm at the studio."

"Well shit, I'm on my way, give me bout forty-five minutes."

"Bet."

The studio was in an affluent upscale neighborhood called Lake Olympia. I pulled into the two-story clubhouse overseeing the lake. I could see Jay upstairs with a few people looking out at the lake listening to music. I waved at Jay to get his attention. He noticed me and yelled,"My mutha fucking nigga!"

He pointed at me, so that the people with him saw me.

"I've been trying to find this nigga since forever! Bring your ass up here!"

I walked in the building and got into the elevator. There were only two floors so I got off on the second. I walked to the receptionist, whom Jay had informed of my arrival.

"Hello, Nation!'
"Hello, Sylvia!"

I replied, as I looked at her name-tag on her desk. Damn she was a beautiful señorita.
"Jay's in the back, just follow where the hallway takes you."
"Okay, beautiful, thank you."

I did as directed and reached the studio area. There was a small crowd assembled about the room and patio. The view of the lake was a sight to see. The setting of the sun only made it even more stunning. Jay approached me.
"Nation, I'm glad you decided to make your presence felt."

We embraced, then he introduced me to the people in the room. Afterwards I followed him to the patio to talk. The first thing I asked was "What the hell happened that day? Because when I heard those gunshots, I jumped out the restroom window! I watched the news that night and it said that everyone in the house got killed. How in the hell did you get out alive!?"

"Nation, when them niggas kicked in the door and started blasting I dove towards the right side of the couch! I crawled to the bedroom and hid under the bed! They never saw me.

Later I found out that it was a hit. They were paid to take down my uncle over some shit he did to some people he didn't think would retaliate. When the smoke cleared and those hitters left, I was the only one left alive. I knew where my uncle's stash was so I grabbed it then shot off.

"Nation, I tell ya when I finally slowed down and counted everything it was close to two bricks and seventeen thousand."

"Got Damn! at fifteen years old?" I asked.

"Hell yeah, my nigga. I shot off like a rocket!"
"I bet you did!"

"Yeah, I plugged in with some major niggas and never looked back. Right now, I'm juggling a nice amount of paper. I fell back because niggas was getting knock. I'm really surprised that them alphabet boys ain't came for me yet. I bought this acre of land and had this studio built about a year ago. This is my refuge. I come to watch the sun's rays dance on the lake's current. It eases my stress."

"I hear you bro, this is beautiful."
"Every now and then you would cross my mind. I'd be like, what happened to my lil' homie Nation?"
"Shit," I countered, "we're back now!"

Jay reached out his hand, we slapped fives then embraced.
"This is the rebirth!"
"Real talk!"

Streets v Fame (33) "Still in me"

"One more push to make it look good,
One more push to get up out the hood,
One more push to make it look right
So we can take flight, for the rest of our life!"

"Yeah, that's the one! Jay shouted, putting two thumbs up.

I came out of the booth to hear how the song sounded on those speakers.

"Yeah, I had to amp up my voice a little bit."
"Yeah, that was perfect." The engineer acknowledged while bobbing his head.

That was the end of our latest session. We trapped ourselves in the studio for a week aiming to create a masterpiece of a mixtape in the same length of time as Jay-z said it took him to create "The Blueprint." We listened to dozens of tracks, vibed with almost a dozen vocalists, and ended up completing thirty-three songs. Out of those songs, seventeen made the cut.

Afterwards, I worked on my solo album, which I named "Rite of Passage" which was from the name of that song we performed years ago at the school's talent show. We decided to name the mixtape we did together "The Allegiance." The first single was called "The Crowning." The first single was put online. We opened up for artists in our area, did videos, and features. Things were moving, but at a snail's pace.

My young hot headed ass couldn't separate the streets from the fame. On the low, I was still running routes across I-10, and up and down 45. I was really only fucking with this music shit because of my nigga Jay. My heart was really with the numbers my plug from the valley was shooting me. Plus, I was secretly at odds with Jay for not plugging me in with his people. He was like,"Bro, I fell all the way back for a reason. I believe in what we are doing, and I don't want to put you in harm's way." The shit sounded like it made sense, but at that time I wanted dollars. I was one track minded like a muthafucka.

I got a call from my nigga Fly in Bryan urging me to fallback because my name had been ringing too loud around the wrong ears. Fly was my nigga and his word was bond but I dismissed his advice because there were only a few niggas in that area that I actually dealt with. I'd known them for a while and they had always been thorough, at least that's what I thought. But when "them people" apply pressure, pipes burst.

Ride or Die Bonnie and Claude (34)

Harmony and I were cooling at my spot when dude hit me on the horn.

"Nation, what's the deal? How you looking?"

"Shit, I'm Straight, what's up?

"Well, shit I need you to come through."

"Yeah, what's the word?"

"A Romo and a split."

"Alright, I'll touch base with you soon."

"Bet."

"Yo, gal. I got some business to attend to, I'll come back soon."

"Mi come too."

"Nah I'm good. I got this mama."

"No!!" She shouted in her yankee voice demanding,"Nigga; I'm coming too!"

"Alright lady, Damn!"

Ignoring Intuition (34) "I can feel it in the air..."

When I got to Bryan, like Beanie Sigel's song "Feel it in The Air," my spidey senses started tingling and I felt it in the air. I should've followed Fly's advice, along with my own intuition, but I didn't. When I pulled onto the dude's street, I hit him on the horn.

"Woe, hey, what's up?"

I saw his car in the driveway but I kept going and made the block.

"Shit, bro I'm at the spot waiting on you."

I still had it on my mind to just leave once I made the block, but instead, I circled back. After a long moment of silence on the phone I mumbled,

"Come outside."

I pulled up against the curb next to the driveway. When I saw the first black Impala hit the corner, I knew what it was. I slowly pulled off to see if my mind was playing tricks on me, but Harmony's gangsta ass put her foot over mine and pressed the gas pedal!

"Drive!"

Harmony yelled, just as another black Charger hit the corner. The chase was on. I cut a few corners trying to make it to the highway, but police cruisers popped up everywhere. They already had a perimeter set up. Not knowing the area, I was doomed from the start. But I ain't give up; I kept pushing through the small town's main street. I made a left on one of the side streets and saw the highway was about half a mile away. I thought to myself, if I can make it to the highway, I may have a chance. I had to be going ninety down that side street and only had a quarter mile to go when they decided to throw the spikes on the street. I saw that and yelled "FUCK!" I had to slow down or get us both killed!

Harmony snatched the steering wheel to the right but it was too late. I ran over the spikes as the Lincoln jolted to the right, making the car flip over two or three times, landing on its roof. We were upside down in the Lincoln when the police drew down on us, yelling to see our hands. They yanked us out of the car, put cuffs on us, and threw us in the back of their cruisers. We went to jail; my Lincoln went to the investigation's custody.

Harmony was later released after I told them she didn't have anything to do with what happened; that she was just along for the ride. They found my stash spot which had the work and banger in it. I was charged with both, along with a host of lesser charges. I couldn't bond out because I had a warrant out for my arrest in Harris County. I got extradited back to Houston for a murder charge.

I stayed in Harris County for over a year fighting those cases. Renae, Jay and my lionesses stood by my side. While in the county, Jay put a few videos we had

done on an underground show called "Street Flavor."
It came on Saturday nights. After a few people saw
those videos, I became a county jail celebrity. That
was a good look, the way Jay whom I had dubbed
"The General" by then, did the interview with
Harmony and Tiara; wearing those "Free Nation" t-
shirts. I eventually beat the murder charge due to lack
of evidence, but I still had to do time for that work and
banger. My lawyer was given another eight-teen grand
so that he could work his muscle. He got me three
years for the "Ross" and the split. The pistol case got
dropped.

Shout out to my lawyer Edward Williams.

The "Flyest Science"/ Supreme Economics (35)

I "caught chain" to Garza East in Beeville, Texas
during the summer. It was hot as hell! A 101 degrees
every day in that muthafucka! You had to condition
your mind to be able to handle that shit, along with
dealing with cornball ass niggas and how they are in
their feelings over petty shit. Plus those police ass
guards that want to write you up for every little thing

like they get a raise for that shit. After going through intake, processing and all that extra shit, UCC transferred me to Ramsey 1 in Rosharon, Texas. It was basically around the corner from Houston which made it easier for me to get visits every week.

I settled in a two-man cell with this old school inmate who was on his way home...He had already done fifteen on a twenty-five for an aggravated robbery. His name was Robert Johnson, an ex-al-Islam Muslim turned Five Percenter. His "knowledge of self" -name was "Supreme Economics" Eco for short.

Eco was one of the smartest dudes I'd ever met. He introduced me to the "Science." Every morning, when the sun rose, he'd be like "Peace God, what's the Science?"

I would have to recite the Science and or Mathematics of that day, according to the knowledge of the Nation of Gods and Earths.

Most of his books were about group economics and financial literacy. We'd be reading "The Wall Street

Journal" and "The Barron's Report" until three in the morning while he taught me how to read stocks. I didn't fully pledge my allegiance to the Five-Percenters, but I adhered to a lot of their science and mathematics.

We were in the cell one night and he was reading a book about the Black Panthers and how J. Edgar Hoover used the co-intelligence program to infiltrate them.

Eco asked "Nation, how did you get that name? Or even Omega for that matter?"

I showed him the birthmark on the lower right side of my neck.

"This looked like the ancient Omega sign to my mother."

"Oh I see it. So how did she come up with your first name?"

"My mother's name is Ebony Lord. She used to talk about how she used to be a part of the Black Panther Party back in the day, how my name meant this and about building a nation within a nation. I never paid attention to most of that shit she was talking about, because she stayed high on crack and that shit disgusted me."

Eco's eyes lit up!

"You're talking about Ebony Nairobi Lord?! I see the resemblance! I remember her-she's an underground legend! Your mother's incarcerated right?"

"Yeah."

"Yeah, I know. She was active in the movement around the same time as Afeni and Assata were in New York. Years ago, I met her at a food drive in Third Ward. She's a very intelligent woman. I remember when she and other Panthers got framed for kidnapping and killing that racist ass judge. Even though she beat the charge, she was ostracized so she had to go underground to survive."

"Damn," I said solemnly; "She never told me that."

"Yeah, that was in the early eighties. The eighties were crazy! That's when the Iran-Contra scandal took place and the U.S. government flooded black communities with crack."

"So you mean to tell me the government really flooded black communities with crack cocaine?"

"Yeah, they used the money from the crack sales to fund the Iran-Contra rebels, who were trying to overthrow the Iranian government."

Amazed I asked, "Are you fucking serious!?"

"As a heart attack!" Eco proclaimed.

"That's fucking crazy!"

"Right. So you dissing your old "Earth" like that, just imagine what she had to deal with coming from being a stand up pillar for the Black Liberation struggle to being forced underground. After the Panthers were decimated, she had to go underground to survive, because no one would hire her and she couldn't get any government assistance. I could imagine the toll it took on her morale being a direct contradiction to who she was and what she stood for. I know because I experienced the same thing as your mother."

"Over our time, here in this wilderness, countless numbers of us have. Dealing with being an ex-con which leads to being dis-enfranchised, marginalized and oppressed to the point where you have to commit various crimes just to survive. I'm not telling you to excuse her addiction, but take all that into consideration. The fact that she had no way to physically escape the despair and hopelessness that surrounded all areas of her life."

I later laid in my bunk, thinking deeply about what Eco said about my mother and gained a new level of respect for her.

Bond Solidified (36)

Once I got into rhythm, time passed a lot faster than it did in Harris County. I trained with the rec rats on a regular basis, sometimes two or three times a day. I would be in the library soaking up knowledge or on the phone most of the time. I also became a vegan in prison for a lil while! Shut up Harmony!

Eco taught me how to invest, trade and short sell stock. I'd call Tiara on a regular basis to make plays for me. But as time passed, I ran into a few obstacles. Between school, studying and working Tiara didn't have it in her to learn how to handle the stock market. I knew Harmony wasn't built like that so I didn't even ask. The next reason was I wanted to be able to check on the market at night. I was interested in trading currencies on the international market and trading on the Shanghai Composite required that you observed that market during their hours. So the time change was the problem. The unit racked up at 10:30 pm U.S. midwestern standard time. On the other side of the world it would be 1:30 p.m.

I ended up solving that problem by buying a "Jag" cell phone. The first time Eco saw me with the "Jag" that night in the cell he warned me, "Sun, you got two to twenty in your hand right there, you overstand?" As I checked the S&P 500 index and made a transaction on TD Ameritrade, I responded, "I overstand, I just want to be able to see my money and be on time to see what the market is doing."

"O.K." he cautioned.

I should've taken heed to Eco's omen, because a short time afterwards I got knocked with the muthafucka. Acting carelessly, I thought I knew what was happening on my block. Around 3 o'clock one day, I anxiously grabbed the "Jag" from the stash spot to check the stock market. What I didn't know was that officers were in the midst of doing random cell searches. So when two guards popped up in front of the cell, I had the "Jag" in my fucking hand in plain view.

"Roll C-7 now!" The first guard yelled. "Got damn!" I uttered to myself in frustration. As the cell doors rolled to open, the guards watched me get up and throw it into the toilet.

As I pushed the button to flush, they rushed in the cell, but the muthafucking "Jag" wouldn't flush! The two guards jammed me up, handcuffed me and took me to lock up. I later found out that the toilet wouldn't flush because they had turned the water off. So what I'd thought was a random shake down, was actually a set up. I stayed in solitary confinement for about forty-five days, awaiting a major case disciplinary court. I was also told I'd be charged with a felony.

The day finally arrived for me to appear in front of the Major, Captain and disciplinary officer. A few minutes into the proceedings, Eco walked through the door accompanied by a Sergeant; Eco asked the Major for a moment of his time. At the time, I didn't know what to think! The Major rose up from his desk and Eco followed him into his office. A few moments passed before they returned.

Eco walked out of the room, while the Major sat back in his-seat at the desk. He looked at me, then opened the folder that held my case file. He looked towards me again for a moment, nodded his head at the disciplinary officer then announced,"Case dismissed." I damn near jumped up out of my skin, once it registered in my mind what he'd said!

I was released from lock up and on my way back to C-7 with my mat on my shoulder and property in my hands. As I waited for C-7 to open I blurted, "Eco Supreme! Peace God!" We then embraced as I walked in the cell.

"Peace Sun," he returned.
"Damn," I announced, "I don't know what you told the Major but hey, I appreciate you God!"

I placed my property in its proper place and took a seat.

"Yeah" Eco said," The Major owed me a favor, I helped him clean up his credit, and got his taxes straight."

"Man, you made my bond!"

"It's nothing, that's what family do for family."

"I just want to know how they knew I had a phone?"

"Nation, that officer you bought the horn from got knocked, then rolled over on you."

A year into my time on Ramsey unit, Eco got released. A few days before he was released, we were "building" in the library. I looked in the history section and found a book on the Civil War and Abraham Lincoln. Eco was sitting at one of the tables reading the USA TODAY newspaper. After I checked the book out, I went and sat next to him.

"Hey, Nation, check this out." He passed me the front page. It was a photo of Black Lives Matter protests over the recent string of cops killing unarmed Black people.

"Yeah, this shit crazy,"I proclaimed, "The racism's real! The system's broken!"

"No," Eco replied. "The system's doing just what it's designed to do.

The system needs to be overhauled, so we can all have an equal playing field."

He gestured towards what I was holding and then asked, "What you got there?"

"A book about the Civil War and Abraham Lincoln."

"Well, here's a little mathematics for you. Follow the money trail.

Like the "Wizard of OZ," follow the yellow brick road. Follow the money to where it leads and you'll see the real reason for about ninety percent of what happens in this world especially when you're dealing with "his-story."

"His-story?!" I shot back laughing.

"Yeah, not history "God," His-tory! They always try to imply that ole Abe freed the slaves, because of some moral act of righteousness, when in fact he emancipated the slaves to break the south."

"Wait a minute Eco, you lost me!"

"Listen God, let me shine some light on you. Those Confederates were grossing millions, if not billions off the backs of Blacks' slave labor. So ole Abe did the math and figured by emancipating the slaves, he would stall the south economically."

"Damn Eco! That makes a lot of sense, once you think about it. Slow the money, how they gonna run it!"

"Like I said God, follow the money. Lincoln said himself that if he could've won the war without freeing the slaves, he wouldn't have freed them. If it wasn't about the money then think about this. During the Emancipation Proclamation, once Lincoln freed the slaves, the newly freed slaves were supposed to be compensated with forty acres and a mule. It's been a century and a half later, and that tab is still running up! What really adds more insult to injury is that to this very day, over 40 million whites and over 240 companies benefit from the labor of our ancestors. That bread didn't just disappear! Check this out, when I get released, I'll send you some more books by this economist named Dr. William Darity. Dude supreme with the "math."

The Highest Truth (37)

That night I went with Eco, to what would be his last time at Jumar, which was a Muslim service. The Nation of Gods and Earths stem from the Islamic tree. And although the Gods were a movement on their own, they still interacted with Islam. Eco was one of the coordinators and speakers on this unit. He wanted to bid farewell to his brothers. Once we greeted everyone, I sat along with the brothers while Eco approached the podium to speak. He opened up with a prayer. "My brothers, you all may know this will be my last night with you all. My time has come, freedom-awaits!"

"Allah o Akbar!" The Muslims chanted.

Eco continued, "I would like to thank you brothers for allowing me to be a part of your community, so I could learn, grow, and flourish into the person I have become today."

The crowd again chanted, "Allah o Akbar!" in response.

"I'm also grateful to have the connections I've been able to obtain, to help me to continue to be an asset to my people once released. Before I depart from this podium for the last time to allow the Imam to speak, I want to leave you all with a little somewhat of a special verse I've written in my personal notes.

It says, "Woe to inhabitants of America, once the children of the damned unite and move as one people, for one cause, regardless of their political, religious, social, organizational, and or gang affiliations. The future is ours to write, remember that."

"Allah o Akbar!"

The Gift (38)

The same day Eco was released was the night King Aswad appeared to me. He hadn't appeared to me since Savage's death. He did appear to my mother which had me tripping because that validated his existence. But that was years ago. I was sitting on the empty bottom bunk, reading one of the Wall Street Journals that Eco had left me when this faint golden glow appeared.

"Long time, no see," I said, once he had fully manifested. The King just nodded his head and smiled.
"You appeared to my mother right?"
He nodded his head again to signify his answer.

"Okay man, what do you want from me?"
"For you to fulfill prophecy. You have great power within you."

"Okay," I expressed sarcastically, "Whatever. So who are you really, and why come to me?"
"You are the direct heir to the throne of the Aswanni Tribe."
"So what, you're saying, you're my ancestor?"
He then gave me the rundown on what happened to the Aswanni Tribe along with the millions

of Africans that had been dispersed and displaced across the globe.

After he finished his story, my mind was blown. I whistled then sighed in amazement.

"Whoa! And you want me to do what?" I asked.

"Unite the remnant of the Aswanni Tribe and fulfill prophecy."

"How am I supposed to do that?"

Aswad raised his golden staff and pointed the head of the staff which had a crown on it towards me as if to "knight me." "I now impart in you the spirit of Rhythm-Mystic Poetry." After knighting me, he tapped the crown of the staff on my forehead, which shot an electric current through my body. I jolted a bit but regained my composure.

"There is someone close to you, who is aware of who you are..." he said, then vanished. I sat for a while, awestruck by what had just taken place. Once the initial shock of what happened subsided my nerves finally calmed down and I dozed off.

I sunk into my dream state; into a semi-sequence of dreams. In the first sequence, I was in what seemed to be a huge church. There was only one person there. A dark chocolate mocha skinned lady, with a veil over her face wearing a wedding dress. She was standing at the altar. At first, I stood stationary, staring at her from afar. The next moment, I was facing her putting a ring on her finger.

In the second sequence, I was somewhere in space. It was like my soul was being transported to some unknown ascended realm. The farther I traveled, the darker It became, to the point where I couldn't see anything in front of me. Pitch Black. There was also another presence I couldn't see but felt. I curiously reached out into the abyss for anything. Then I felt something, a breast. I continued to lightly touch this body and noticed that I was being touched also. As this woman and I continued touching each others' intimate parts I realized that we were both naked. While I tried to comprehend what was going on, I felt the woman's lips press against mine.

There we began the ancient ritual of love making. She grabbed my aroused manhood and placed it inside of herself. Once intertwined, "I rocked her boat" sensually, until I released my seed then I awoke.

The ghetto's got a mental telepathy (39)

The spirit of Rhythm-Mystic Poetry is the ability to speak, rhyme, or sing as well as decipher the deeper esoteric meanings and higher truths that are revealed in the lyrics, the beat of the drums and melodies. After being touched by King Aswad's staff, I began to "overstand" hip-hop at its highest heights. I theorized that there had to be others who pierced the veil to bring in the light. The questions I posed to myself were:

"Were they initiated into some sort of fold?
"Did they go through levels?
"Were they touched by King Aswad?"

Time to Think (40)

Besides the literature Eco left me, I acquired my own collection which I had my team, whom I dubbed at that time "Omega Guard," sent me.

There were books on subjects such as Politics, Economics, Psychology and also Health and Fitness. Some of the books I had sent were about the Constitution, the Bill of Rights and the three branches of the government. I dug into them like I was Huey P. Newton. Also, I obtained books on stocks, day trading, hedging, options, securities and so forth.

Most of all, I fell in love with ancient history. The history of ancient Kemet-Egypt and Kush-Ethiopia, reading about Akhenaten and Nefertiti, the dynasties that were created, their religions, concepts, and ideologies. Literature from archaeologists like Ivan Van Sertima, Cheikh Anta Diop, John Henry Clarke, Dr. Yosef Ben Jochannan, Dr. Claude Anderson, Tony Browder, the list goes on! To this day, I still have those books on my shelf. Some of those books were a deciding factor in my son's Omega entering the field of law. I keep them as a reminder of those times of my development in the belly of the beast…America.

Unconditional Love (41)

That Saturday, Harmony came to visit me. As usual, her outfit took my breath away. A black Saint Laurent shirt with a lion imprint and black leather pants to match. She came to the table. We embraced, kissed and sat across from each other.

"Yo gal," I said in my best impersonation of a yard-man I could manage while reaching to hold her hand.

She gave me her hand and responded, "Yo my lion, waa gwaan?"
"I'm cool lady. I'm missing the world though. What's up with it out there?"

"Same thing," she says slyly, "Your yankee wife, Tiara soon graduates. Jay's pushing y'all's toons. Renae said she'll be here next week."

"I heard Harvey tore the city up?"
"Yeah, half the city got flooded, it's a mess."
"How was Renae's neighborhood?"
"It wasn't damaged too much, her home is ok."

She had a ring on her thumb. She pulled it off of her thumb and handed it to me. I surveyed it and asked,"What's this for?"

"Boy, shut up!" she snapped. "And put this on one of your fingers!"

I put it on my pinky finger to see if it would fit. It was a Bvlgari diamond ring with VVS cuts. I took a look at how it looked on my fingers.

"Yeah, this is nice. I like this."

She held out her pinkie which had a ring on it too. I instinctively reached for her pinkie to interlock my own.

She said,"This is to us, till the end of time, no matter what."

"Till the end of time," I responded.

We went back to holding each other's hand for a silent moment when I asked,"How long have you known?"

Raising one eyebrow, she replied, "Known what?"

See the thing with Harmony is, she rarely shows her feelings, she keeps her screw face on. You really have to know her to be able to read her. When she slightly released her hands from mine, I knew she was the one King Aswad was referring to. So I pressed on.

"King Aswad. He appeared to you, didn't he?"

"Yes lion," she purred. "That weekend you and Tiara went to visit your mother, Tiara told me what your mother said about King Aswad. Mi thought it was hilarious until he appeared to me that night.

"Wait? What happened, did he say anything?"

"He told me about you, about us as a people, and bout how mi been here before."

With a puzzled and astounded look I asked, "What!?"

"Him put his fingers on my forehead and memories of my past life emerged. I was Aswanni royalty, I was an ambassador."

"Whoa, that's crazy!" I was amazed.

"Yes lion, Mi rode with King Aswad on his diplomatic tours to unite the tribes of Africa." I thought my mind was blown before!

I asked,"Did you move down here to Houston to watch over me? I felt that was going on but I dismissed that thought because at that time I thought I was going insane!"

Flashback: 1571 A.D. (42) Iyanna/ Harmony

In the year 1571, King Aswad became the head chieftain of the seven tribes who were the head tribes that surrounded the area that is now known as Senegal. It was an elaborate tribal system which had checks and balances. Each tribe produced a major resource which was traded across the continent. This made these particular tribes collectively the most wealthy tribes on the continent at that time.

When King Aswad received the gift of Rhythm-Mystic Poetry, then commissioned to use it to unite the continent, Kwannzia held reservations on how to do it. Harmony, whose name was Iyanna at the time, ran down to me what she remembered from her past life after King Aswad resurrected her memories.

"Mi remembered mi loved going with Aswad on these journeys. He was a wise, kind and humble man who believed in unity. Although Kwannzia was my biological father, I considered Aswad my spiritual father. I watched how he dealt with people, handled conflicts and delegated power. Aswad was very charismatic, he was guiding light to those who searched for meaning.

On the other hand, my father Kwannzia was very hard, dominating and strong willed. My father and Aswad may have had their differences politically, but they were like brothers, or so I thought.

They were both initiated in the ancient mystical arts of Apex Omega, which I heard was a form of Aswannan ancestral worship intertwined with ancient Northern Buddhism that dates back at least two millennia. The secrets that Aswanna held were known only to these Buddhist monks.

While Aswad excelled in the arts, my father gravitated to becoming a fierce warrior. Aswad rose to become King of Aswanna and Kwannzia became General. The split came between the two over their ideological ideas about uniting the continent. My father wanted to trade resources and acquire weapons of war with the newly acquainted European foreigners so that he could take the continent by force. He wanted to rule with an iron fist. He felt it would be better to be feared than loved. Aswad wanted to unite the continent the way his ancestors directed him. He wanted to wait and deal with the Europeans after he united and fortified the continent.

Months before Aswad was assassinated, I overheard them having a heated discussion on how to wield power, when my father pulled a knife on Aswad. Aswad's guards had to stop him. I had my suspicions once my father took the throne after Aswad's death. But then my father was killed by the foreigners. They invaded and imprisoned us, then loaded us on ships and shipped us off. We rebelled on the ships but were overpowered when they started shooting us. They murdered mi brothers and raped mi sisters. I wouldn't allow them to touch me... so I jumped to my death in the Atlantic.``

That was the reason Aswad didn't want to trade with foreigners at that time. He had seen the multiple futures that awaited our people. In order to become the Highest Esoteric Monk in the ancient mystical order of Apex-Omega, he had to learn and recite verbatim the Aswannan Buddhist oracles. Those oracles contained the history of Aswanna's past, present and possible paths to the future. But with the death of Aswad, the prophecies pertaining to Aswanna and the African continent was considered to be just legend. Aswad confirmed to Harmony what she suspected of his assassination when he appeared to her. He assured her he had no ill feelings towards her, because he knew what had happened between him and her father.

Harmony was pure-hearted, which is why the ancestors in the spiritual realm decided to reincarnate her. The universal esoteric energies combined with the will of our ancestors, brought Harmony and I together in Atlanta... so we were destined to meet.

Prophecy (43)

I had one more day in prison before I would be released. That night King Aswad appeared to me again. At the time I was reading a book about leadership. This was one of the books I had Harmony sent to me. Once he fully manifested, I noticed he was smiling. Out of the deep love, reverence and admiration that grew within me, after learning about how he'd sacrificed his life for his people, I knelt before him. He looked down at me.

"Arise my son, don't fret. You are destined for greatness." Aswad was draped in all kinds of diamonds, gold, platinum, onyx and sapphire filled medallions around his neck, arms and wrist.

As I rose up, he grabbed a medallion that resembled a cross with twelve points and took it off his neck. We stood face to face. He placed the cross on my forehead then announced,"I'm imparting the spirit of prophecy within you, my son." The cross sent an electrical charge through my body that jolted my soul.

I was instantly transported to what seemed to be some sort of rehabilitation center. A gorgeous dark mocha-skinned pregnant woman was sitting at a desk next to a bed. I spoke to the woman as if I already knew her, asking how she was doing. She seemed to be at ease with me being there because she showed no fear. As I continued to physically talk to her, I was also having a duel conversation in mind that went like this:

"What the fuck am I doing here?"

Out of nowhere, a second voice stated, "You're searching for hidden treasure and she's a jewel."

"Wait, what?" I shot back, "Who the fuck is this in my mind?"

"I'm you," the voice answered, "Your consciousness from the future, year 2045."

"Woe!" The present version of myself said in amazement. "So we travel through time in our minds in the future!?"

"Yea, but that's another story, for another time. For now, let me work my muscle, because I only have a certain amount of time. She's an important part of Aswanna's future.

When the future version of myself said that, I faded to black, and let him take control. I then mentally returned my focus to the conversation my future self was having with this woman.

"Black Nationalistic Ascension Codes? I'm curious, you have my attention Ms. Scott."

"Yes," she replied, "Besides teaching the standard reading, writing and math. I feel for the next three to four generations, we should devote ourselves to teaching our youth what I've dubbed as our Ascension Codes. Which are politics, economics, science and nationhood. We should teach these Ascension Codes to our youth as early as possible. So that our youth could develop the mindset of organizational self sufficiency that is needed for us to progress as a people."

"I'm with you on that angel."

"In addition; I'm working on compiling a thesis that I've called "Hip Hop, The True Black Religion."

"Yea," my future self commented, "It is a way of life."

"Yes it is!" she asserted. "It's the way we walk, talk, dress, move, think, communicate; it's our culture. One of the reasons I'm compiling this thesis is because

I feel for Hip Hop to be a long lasting superior force for our people, it should be regulated."

"I don't totally agree with you on that part but I do understand."

This conversation kind of puts me in the mind of what Andre 3000 said on a song with Jeezy called "I Do," when he says:

"Maybe 2030
 our baby she'll be nerdy."
"I commend you for even having the mental capacity to think on that level."

She turned in her chair and gestured to my future self to help her up. I, meaning we assisted her when she paused once she rose. Just as she was beginning to gently glide her fingers across my face, something within my spirit began to stir. I started to have that same shocking feeling I did once I got touched by King Aswad's medallion. My future self urgently puts two fingers on her eyes and declared,

"See the future, for Aswanna! Ok!"

I awoke on the ground the next morning sore as hell on some quantum leap shit.

Free at Last (44)

When I got released from the Walls unit, the General was standing outside next to a limo waiting for me. Harmony hopped off the limo's hood and ran into my arms.

"Oh my lion! You're out!" She purred as she hugged then kissed me.
"Damn gal! I missed you."

Once we released the grip we had on each other, I slapped fives with the General and embraced him.
"Whats up my nigga?"
"Shit, I'm free!"

He looked at me then at the clothes I had on then said, "Come on, let's go get you fresh to def, cause this shit here ain't working!" We all hopped in the limo and headed to the Galleria mall. I followed the General to the Louis Vuitton store.

"Ay, Nation, get you something fresh, because we gone get our grown man on tonight."

I got a few pairs of Louis Vuitton fits, a watch and chain. Then we went to Neiman Marcus to grab some Gucci and Fendi outfits. Afterwards we pulled into the Hotel Derek. Harmony had already booked a room there.

"Nation, get yourself together, because we gone ball tonight!"
"That's a bet, big bro!"

I embraced and saluted the General, grabbed my bags and got out of the limo. Harmony and I walked into the hotel. While we were in the lobby, Harmony handed me her phone.

"Here, child," she said slyly.
I grabbed the phone to speak. "Woe now!" All I heard was screaming over the phone.

"Baby, you're home!"

"Hey, now classy lady, what's up?"

"Nation, I'm at the airport terminal. I should be in Houston around nine p.m. So don't let Harmony wear you out!" she said as we both laughed.

I replied, "I'm not, babe!"

Real Love (45)

When we arrived in the room, I took a shower and put on the Louis Vuitton suit with the watch and chain. I looked in the mirror and thought to myself, "Damn, it's good to be out."

"Hey, how do I look?"

Harmony stood behind me for a second and examined how I looked in the mirror. She walked up behind me, wrapped her arms around me and replied, "My lion, you look like my king."

I turned to face her and said, "Yo gal, you gotta stop doing that!"

"Stop what?" she asked.

I grinned and answered, "Gassing me up!"

She kissed me. "But you are, no?"

So Flashy, Jazzy, and Classy (45) "Luxurious"

Later that night, Jay the General came back and scooped us up in the limo.

I asked, "Hey, I thought Tiara was going to be with you?"
"Nah, she's going to meet us later."

We passed through a variety of spots, lounges, strip clubs, and bars around the city, linking up with people who welcomed me home. The last place we landed was a place called Sophi's Chateau Bar and Lounge.

The General put his arm around my shoulder and expressed as we stepped in; "Yeah, this is where we need to be, where the power players of the city are. City councilman, judges, lawyers, even the mayor." The place was packed. We took our reserved seats at a table in the middle facing the stage where the live band was doing their thing. Just as I was about to ask if anyone heard from Tiara, a familiar voice began humming in a soft, soothing tone throughout the lounge. Once she appeared, she sashayed on the stage. She looked luxurious rocking her Hermes top and skirt which matched Manolo boots and gloves.

She continued to croon as the piano weaved an angelic melody that blended beautifully with her voice. I was stunned by how elegantly she maneuvered on stage.

"Asia!" I announced surprisingly as I tilted the glass of Bordeaux in my hands toward Harmony, Jay, and Renae who had just shown up. "Y'all knew about this, didn't you!" They all smiled back, as Tiara carried on MC-ing.

"Hello, Midtown Lounge. My name is Asia Tiara Richards, also known as Tiara Sky. I'd like to celebrate life with you all tonight—a celebration of love, a celebration of freedom and a celebration of power!" She swung into her song and enchanted the crowd. Once finished, she received a standing ovation. Afterwards she caught me off guard.

"I would like to introduce to you all a very special acquaintance of mine." She pointed to me.

"Nation, Come to the stage, baby!" I thought to myself, damn she put me on the spot. I swallowed the rest of the Bordeaux, got up then walked to the stage. We embraced and kissed, afterwards one of the band members handed me a microphone.

Tiara then continued, "Can you all please give a warm welcome to Nation Omega Lord!"

The band transitioned to another melody that featured more piano, flutes, and violins. Now that I think back, the melody reminds me of the song "Halo" from Beyonce. Later, I found out that Tiara had informed the band of my taste. It had been a while since I'd rapped and even longer since I'd performed, so I was a little timid once I began MC-ing.

"I thank you all for allowing me," I said while slyly smirking at Tiara, "to celebrate life with you all tonight. I'm truly appreciative." Once I caught the rhythm, I elegantly transitioned into the verse:

"From the depths of my soul,
I dug deep within myself to find that gold,
Raised in the streets where it's dark and cold,
That seed burst through concrete to grow,

wounds from my past haunt my days,
I still think of Savage when I see Renae,
Those Karats on that ring got stains on them,
I can still feel my ancestors' pain on them.."

Remembering Savage brought a tear to my eye. I recall glancing at Renae as I said that bar and seeing that spirit of unconditional love, which shook me even more.

"You got to excuse me Midtown Lounge, I was kind of caught off-guard with this one."
Someone in the crowd yelled, "You're doing fine baby, keep going!"

Tiara began harmonizing beautifully, which brought out the ambiance of "class" I wanted to convey. Once again I smoothly transitioned onto the verse when the baseline dropped.

"Through corridors of time,
The significance, of events, speaks to minds,
And hearts when I talk, I stimulate the thoughts,
To commemorate what was lost,
Ay, this is the day, we liberate souls held captive,
Free to be who we are, look what happened,

We create something massive
 with such heart and passion,
It's much more than they can imagine,
Looking towards the horizons,
I know that the world is surprised that,
A young leader even survived it
Here I stand, next to footprints in the sand,
I was taught while being carried,
Taught how to be legendary,
Is any of you people ready,
 to be led by the ones with the gift to lead,
A pioneer in my own rite; I see it all in the twilight,
We gone pursue this till it gets right,
From nightfall till the daylight,
 These are the phases of my life...."

While I continued to lyrically serenade the crowd,
Tiara harmonized like an angel. When we finally
finished, the crowd chanted "Encore!" We grabbed
each other's hand and bowed before the crowd,
receiving a standing ovation. Tiara and I departed the
stage and embraced Harmony, Jay and Renae while a

146

crowd circled us, giving compliments, praise, and well wishes. It was truly an exhilarating night.

Never cease to amaze me (46)

I was awakened the next morning by kisses from Tiara, in her room at the Hilton.

"Good morning, Nation," she serenaded seductively in my ear, as she handed me a mimosa while I rose up in bed.
"Morning classy lady," I replied then took a sip of the mimosa.
"That was one hell of a first day out! How long have you been singing and performing like that? Shit, you blew my mind!"

Tiara answered, "One night, a while back, I was chilling at the studio, listening to y'all's music and I started fooling around. Jay liked what he heard, so we just went from there."

"So you mean to tell me, you just woke up like that?!"

"No child please! I've been singing for years, but just for fun. I never took it seriously until I started recording with Jay. Look."

She grabbed her phone and typed in "Tiara Sky in the studio" on YouTube, and videos popped up. She handed me her phone, and I sat for the rest of the morning, completely stunned, watching videos of Tiara.

Down to Business (47)

Those next three months were strictly business. I mean, we really got down to business. I had never been that focused in my life. I personally knew what was at stake. The Omega Guard album that was created was a masterpiece. We agreed to name it "The Rebirth." The photoshoot for the album cover was epic. It was shot at a club parking lot. It featured the Omega Guard team, plus the people who were there to party that Saturday night.

Tiara was wearing a wedding dress and holding a baby in the air while the rest of us surrounded her. The graphic designer made the baby appear to be glowing. The baby's aura emanated from the baby's body and shined on the rest of us. We also did photoshoots in various places throughout the city and in front of the green screen. That was the first time I had seen the twelve-point star-cross Jay created to be our emblem. It reminded me of the cross King Aswad used to impart those gifts within me.

The General and I watched while my lionesses took their photos. The photos of Harmony and Tiara were amazing! The strength and power that they exuded, combined with what they wore signified a new level of class, style, and pizzazz. Their ensembles resembled military-style attire woven with royalty. In my mind, those outfits brought out their personalities. "Damn Nation," Jay shot out, "I don't know what kind of spell you put on these girls but –"

I laughed then responded, "Shit, a spell on them!? They put a spell on me! You wanna see a queen, look I got two. I can't lose with two queens on the chessboard. The crazy thing is they chose me! Shits like a fairytale!"

Jay slapped fives with me, then declared, "My nigga if you got two queens that make you King! King Nation!"

"King Nation?" I pronounced, trying to see how it sounded. "That does have a nice ring to it! The king has arrived, niggas pay yo tithes!"

King Nation featuring Tiara Sky (48)"Pure Heart" video shoot

The video started with us levitating in the sky together as she sang and I rhymed:

"I'm the Buddha, I'm the future
I'm the reason, solar flares are shooting
Born in space-city, better known as Houston
Solar-powered, this is ours, we created a movement..."

As we descend toward Earth, anything that's destroyed, polluted, or desolate was replenished, cleaned or rebuilt. Tiara and I land in downtown Houston. Harmony walks to me, with a crown in her hand. Once she reached me, I bowed my head for her to crown me. We all walked through the city together while I resumed rhyming. Time fast forwards to night. As night falls protestors gather on one side of the street while the National Guard is on the other.

As Tiara starts her verse, I walk up to the National Guard and salute them. The protestors get angry and restless as an armored truck speeds up the street and pulls up to the protestors. I open the armored truck's rear door then hop in. A moment later, I came out holding a big black confetti gun. While I aim the gun in the air towards the protestors the roof of the armored truck opens and two huge canons protract on the left and right side of the roof. I shoot cash in the air and simultaneously do the canons. The protest turns into a party.

"It turns the protest into a party nigga
It's just what the king ordered hear me..."

Promo-Tour (49)

The General immediately went to work on promoting, marketing and booking promo-shows. The promo tour began on New Year's Night in Atlanta. After closing out the show, we were all heading out to the parking lot when we all heard someone yelling out my name. I turned around to see who it was. Top Star! Top had a group of niggas following behind him, which turned out to be his soldiers.

"What's up Nation? How long has it been, like five years!"

We embraced each other and then he approached Harmony.

"What's up shorty, long time no see!"
    "Waa gwaan, my youth!? You still ah flex with Dre-Bo?"
    "Fo-Sho!" Top replied, "That's for life!"

I introduced him to the General and Tiara.

"Hey, this Top Star, the dude I did that mix for Harmony back in the day."

"Oh yeah, I remember that. How are you?" Tiara asked as Jay greeted him.

Top carried on, "Those were some real classical hits, y'all dropped tonight."

"I appreciate you Top," I answered modestly.

"So, what 's going on?"

"Shit, you know me, rapping and trapping!" he replied while laughing.

Why'd it been years since we'd linked up, was because while I was doing that three-year bid, he had already been gone two years prior to me beginning my sentence. He had just recently been released from doing close to eight years for a couple aggravated assaults with a deadly weapon. While in prison, his reputation as a monster and incredible lyricist, among other things, helped him rise in the ranks of the Blood gang to become one of their leaders.

"You say you're still plugged in with Dre-Bo right?"

"Hell yeah! As a matter of fact, we were on our way there now."

I looked at my team and asked, "What's up y'all want to go?"

They all said yea in unison.

"Alright Top put Dre-Bo on the phone and let Harmony holla at him."

Top-Star (50)

When we arrived Harmony and I greeted Dre-Bo then introduced Tiara and The General. We settled in and began listening to some of Dre-Bo's latest tracks. Jay was vibing with Dre-Bo. His latest tracks had that beautiful melodic sound we were looking for. One of his tracks was so classy, I passed him a few thousand right then to purchase it. The most familiar beat that I could tell you put me in the mind of was "Take Advantage" by Ricky Rozay and Future, on that Black Dollar mix-tape. I juggled a few bars, just playing around. Out of the blue, it became a whole song, after

Tiara and Top Star blessed the track. Those few bars I juggled went like:

"When Tiara sings,
It's like freedom rings,
It's a beautiful dream,
To have a beautiful team,
I bought both my queens,
Two diamond rings,
Give me time, they'll see,
I'll buy an island, a piece..."

Top Star pulled out a blunt and fired it up. After taking a couple of puffs, he tried to hand it to me. I declined the offer which surprised him.

"Oh, you don't fuck with the smoke no more?"

"Naw man," I answered, "I'm on some more shit right now. I switched up my whole regimen.

I realized I can't do what other people do, and still be the best I can be. Some people can smoke, some people can drink. I understand that I can't do either and be the leader with the precise decision making skills that I have when I'm sober."

"That's some real shit, Nation," Top expressed as he took another draw of the smoke.

"But you see me" he continued while laughing, "I'mma get high till I die!"

We both had a quick laugh, as he passed the smoke to Harmony.

"Say, Nation."

"What's up?"

"On that song you were spitting at the club, you said some fly shit about the spirit of an ancient, what? What was it you said?"

"I said, I got the spirit of a king who leads me, that's how I'm able to keep ascending."

"Yeah, that's it. What inspired you to come up with some shit like that?"

I exhaled, then replied, "That's some inside shit young."

"The reason I asked is because when I heard those few bars it shot me back to that night we hooked up and traded bars."

"What happened?" I asked puzzled.

"When we were in those booths, I looked at the crowd, and within the crowd, I saw some crazy ass shit that had me thinking I was tripping."

"What did you see?"I asked, eyebrows raised in amazement.

"I saw a spirit. The nigga was all jeweled up. He looked like some king. What's even more crazy is that after that night, ever so often the nigga be in my dreams."

Top noticed how I looked at him then asked, "You saw it too didn't you?"
"Yeah."
"Shit! I knew it wasn't the liquor and "Loud" talking!"
"That spirit you've seen is the spirit of an ancient King named Aswad from the Aswanna tribe."

I gave him the rundown of what I knew about the situation. It blew his mind.

I continued,"Yeah, I don't know what all the dreams mean but I do know that it's gone be some epic shit!"

"So where y'all headed to next?"

"To D.C. We got a lil buzz out there. Plus the General's uncle is the mayor, he is supposed to introduce the team to him."

"You talking bout that nigga running for president? Benjamin Sutton?"
"Yeah. Damn if you ain't busy, you can come with us."
"Alright. Let me check my schedule." He glanced at his cellphone for a split second.
"Shit, looks like I'm free!"
"Nigga you crazy!" I countered, as we burst out laughing.

Mayor Benjamin (51)

We arrived in D.C around three and made it to Jay's uncle's campaign rally just as he wrapped up his speech. He shook hands, took photos and talked with people. Jay waved at him to get him to notice; once he did he weaved his way through the crowd to get to us.

"Hey nephew, I'm glad you were able to make it. How are you doing?"

"I'm okay, Unc."

He glanced at the rest of us. "So this is your team?"

"Yeah," Jay answered, "This is the Omega Guard."

"Are any of you hungry? Because I'm starving, I know a great soul food restaurant where we can go and talk."

Linked to Prophecy (52)

The General introduced us to his uncle Mayor Benjamin as we sat at the table and ordered. Moments later our food arrived.

"I love this place. It has a real down South feel to it. I've been coming here for years." He took a bite of food and continued, "So, Nation my nephew told me, you two grew up together and have been making music since you both were teenagers."

"Yeah, we're pretty much like brothers."
"I've heard some of your music from the latest album called the "Rite of Passage" right?
"Yes sir, that's it."
"You sure have matured a lot from earlier releases. You've always had that class and charisma, but this latest album is just whew! Magnificent!"
"I really appreciate that, especially coming from someone of your caliber."

"While you were away, I can imagine you did a lot of soul-searching and brainstorming. It reminds me of a quote from Malcolm X, which says:

"I put prison second to college as the best place for a man to go if he needs to do some thinking."

"Yes sir, I did a lot of self-evaluating as well as studying."

"And if you don't mind me asking. What's the most important thing you've learned?"

"Sir, don't take what I'm going to say personally, but what I've learned is much more than you can even imagine."

"Oh you think so, huh?" He asked while taking a bite of his food. As he chewed he seemed to be in deep thought. He then asked,"Nation, it's coming to pass, isn't it?" I looked up from the food I was eating but didn't respond.

Jay with a puzzled look asked,"Unc, what are you talking about?"

"Oh, Nation knows what I'm talking about, don't you? I wonder who else has paid attention to your lyrics and link them to prophecy?"

Lineage (53)

Jay was unaware of the prophecy of the Aswanni people because he nor Tiara were from our lineage. We'd all heard of the legend as kids, in bits and pieces, but it's basically just a bedtime story for most of us. Mayor Benjamin, who was Jay's uncle by marriage, was a direct descendent of the Aswanni. He invited us to his home; there would be people there he wanted us to meet. We agreed to meet with him the next night because we had already had a promo show booked for that previous night.

Coalition (54)

The next night at the Mayor's home or should I say mansion, which was a fifteen-bed room, eleven bathrooms, sitting on a hundred-plus acres. They were at least seven Lincoln Continentals and eight limos parked alongside the cul-de-sac and his home. Following Jay through the double doors into the foyer, there had to be at least forty people in attendance. People who were lawyers, politicians, business moguls, military officials, doctors, professors, entertainers, all of whom I vowed not to name. That night my assumptions were confirmed concerning Hip Hop artists who were part of a secret order and who were initiated in this science of "Rhythm - Mystic Poetry."

After being greeted by everyone, he motioned for me to follow him down the hallway. While walking, I noticed the photos on the wall of Civil Rights leaders, political figures, and businessmen, along with pictures of him with power move makers of this era. He also had statues, totem poles and artifacts of antiquity. As I followed him to what looked like a library and or office lobby, I didn't know what to expect. He stood outside the entrance and gestured for me to step in. I took a step just within the entrance. There was an elderly lady sitting in a rocking chair to the right of the library, next to a window. She had on a long beautiful burgundy ole timely dress with slippers to match. There was a book on her lap, but at that moment she was looking out the window into the night's sky. The full moon's light shined on her face, making her appear majestic.

When she finally turned to face me, my heart skipped a beat. But not out of fear, it was due to the overwhelming power she exuded. I was awestruck! She smiled then proclaimed, "At last! I have been allowed to be in the presence of our king before I meet my ancestors!" Her voice was like a multitude of people's voices speaking at once. In that split second, it seemed that everyone of my ancestors' souls spoke through her. It was amazing! As she adjusted her glasses to see me, she gestured for me to come closer. I approached her and knelt before her. Tears welled up in my eyes as I spoke, "King ma'am? I'm no king, I'm just Nation."

She grasped my face, raised it towards her then replied, "Don't be wary or afraid of what our ancestors have ordained. Take heart, my son. The time has come for you to break the yoke of bondage off of our people's neck." A crowd formed around us. From within the crowd a young woman approached me, while I was still kneeling before the elderly woman. She put her hand on my shoulder then stated, "We've all been having these dreams and visions that we've been trying to make sense of."

I rose and stood next to the elderly woman, while I held her hand for comfort. Standing in her presence, I felt a sense of nostalgia, a longing for something I had never experienced myself. It was as though that feeling was being transferred from her to me. It dawned on me what that feeling was. It was a feeling of true freedom. Then I thought to myself, how old was this woman?

I turned towards the crowd to address them. "Ever since my first encounter with the spirit of King Aswad, I've always felt as though I was somehow losing my mind. Now I know that I'm not alone, I feel rejuvenated. And I'm truly thankful for all of your support." Mayor Ben approached me from within the crowd and announced, "These dreams and visions you all have been having are an indication of the fact that we are on the eve of an ancient prophecy that's yet to be fulfilled... that is an oracle of the African people.

The reason you all have been having these visions is because you all are direct descendants of the Aswanni tribe. The Aswanni people were the bearers and still are of the spiritual manifestation of Rhythm-Mystic Poetry, which is today's Hip-Hop. So in essence the Aswanni people remain the vanguards of this prophecy."

Top's crazy ass joking around asked, "I just wanna know, do we have to call Nation your Highness now!" I slapped fives with Top ass as we laughed. "Top, you stupid!"

Breakfast Club (55)

Continuing on the promo tour, we traveled to Baltimore, Cleveland, Cincinnati, Philly, and New Jersey. While in New York, the General plugged in with Charlemagne tha God at the Breakfast Club radio station.

"Yeah, this Charlamagne tha God, and I'm here with the Omega Guard, label mates, King Nation and Jay the General.

What's up, how are you brothers doing?" Jay and I returned greetings.

"I like these brothers, they got the internet buzzing right now. So if you haven't checked them out yet, you need to get to it. As a group, the Omega Guard dropped two albums around the New Year, right?"

"Yeah," Jay replied, "There's a group album with me, Tiara and Nation called the Rebirth. Then Nation released a solo called "Rite of Passage."

"I listen to both albums and both are on my regular playlist. On my iPhone, while I'm driving, working out, meditating or whatever. The music is transcendent. And it has a real regal feel to it."

"I appreciate that. We aimed to keep the energy of the music on an elevated level, as well as a trans-generational level. We want to be able to relate to everyone, from eighteen to eighty. Politically, socially, culturally, and mentally, you know what I mean?"

"Yeah, and my opinion is that y'all did a hell of a job. But there's something, I just have to ask you, Nation."

"What's that?"

"You released The Rite Of Passage, New Year's Day, right?"

"Yeah."

"Then how in the hell did you know that Rodney Simmons would get gunned down by police in Dallas in March? You said and I quote:

"Lil Simmons got riddled, with twenty, in the triple D

woke niggas out of their sleep, on Oak Cliff streets"

Jay was like, "Wow!"

"But that's not it. On another song called "The Shrine" you rhymed about the exact location of the ancient Egyptian Pharaoh Ahkenaton's crown! Archaeologists actually used your lyrics to find the crown! When I saw that on the internet, I went ballistic!

"That was epic! Explain to me. No explain to the world, how in hell you knew that?!"

"Okay wait a minute," I humbly stated then continued, "Listen, God, when I'm in the booth, I just close my eyes and the spirit guides me."

"Let the spirit guide you? So what, you don't write your music?"

"Like I said, I close my eyes and let the spirit guide me."

"So what are you saying like a prophet or something?"

"No, I'm just saying I do what comes naturally."

Midwest (56)

After the interview with Charlemagne Tha God, at the Breakfast Club, we flew to the "Windy City." When we arrived in Chi-Town the whole city was on edge. It was over a highly publicized case where under-covers ran up on a suspected drug dealer and drew down on this young dude named Coese McNeil. Fearing that he might be in the process of being robbed, he pulled his weapon in self-defense. Shots rang out with him shooting one of the three officers. He was also wounded in the ordeal, but the killing part was he had his fifteen-month-old daughter in the backseat who died at the scene. What made it just as bad was that he wasn't even the suspect, they had received bad intel.

McNeil was sent to the hospital treated for his wounds, then locked up for attempted capital murder. If it wasn't for civil rights leaders and social activists bringing his situation to light, the law would have railroaded him and swept it under the rug. There were people like Common, Lupe, Chance the Rapper, and even Obama voicing their concern over this miscarriage of justice.

The whole country was watching to see if the state's attorney general would indict the cops on the murder of McNeil's daughter. That night we were scheduled to perform, you could feel the electricity in the air. Word had traveled via the internet about the interview we'd had at the Breakfast Club, so the place was packed. We were the third group to do a set. Once we mounted the stage, the crowd rushed the stage with their phones on video recording. Tiara and I performed "Pure Heart," from the Rebirth album,"Back to the Money," with the General and a few more songs. Plus one I had recently recorded with Top Star called "Our Time."

We finished our set, and as we were exiting the stage, the crowd started chanting my name! I turned back towards the center of the stage and shouted through the mic.

"Windy City, land of the real leaders, what's up!" the crowd went berserk! We know the city'll a set it off! Like the prophet Tupac said years ago,
   "We might fight amongst each other, but I promise you this,
      we'll burn this bitch down, you get us pissed!"
   After that quote, it seemed like the roof came off!

"But I do have a grievance with my leaders. All this displaced aggression should be aimed at oppression. The same reason for the ongoing economic civil war you're having in this city is the same reason for the disparities we all are facing across the country. Lack of equity, Lack of resources, lack of opportunities, and options, the list goes on. So while we've purposely been distracted fighting this economic civil war for nickels and dimes, this country owes niggas at least twenty trillion! Like the great chairman Bobby Seale of the Black Panthers, stated years ago, "Seize the time!" Channel your energy towards the source of these disparities! Plan, plot, and strategize! If we are to raise our Black nation, reparations are due! Let's build something legendary, so we can leave a helluva legacy!"

Continuing our trek, like the Tribe called Quest, towards the west; I swore I was being followed. But I never said anything because I thought my mind was playing tricks on me. I thought Harmony knew because for one, she'd become an expert at reading my emotions and mannerisms, and how they dictated my actions. The second reason I believed she had a feeling about how I felt was because in every city we landed after Chicago, Top Star and her would always pop up out of nowhere with bangers!

After performing in Los Vegas, the decision was made to drive the rest of the way to Los Angeles. The General rented a Mercedes Benz Sprinter bus and on our way on we went. During the drive, the conversation was brought up about who were the greatest Hip Hop artists of all time. Top Star was doing all this ranting and raving about who he felt was the top five.

Although he had a worthy lineup of artists, I told him this:

"Top it's not as simple as you think. There are categories and levels to this shit. Like for instance, who was the most influential, or who was the most lyrical, or who had the best delivery."

"Not to mention," Jay interjected, "Who sold the most albums or who held the crown the longest."

"Nation, fuck all that intellectual shit!"

Top continued, "You're just trying to curve the question!" Everybody said their top five except you! Spit it out!" he commented as we all laughed. "I'll tell you what," I shot back, "I'll give you my two top fives, team one and team two. Better still, I'll give you the top five of the beginning of the millennium era and of this current era.

"But before I do, I want to bring this into consideration."

"Aww man," Top countered, "You're killing me!"

"Let my baby talk!" Harmony yelled while laughing.

"Thank you, Harmony!" I asserted then continued, "Hip Hop is a sport, but it's not like per-se basketball where statistics plays a major role in who we consider the best. Hip Hop is more abstract and subjective so we consider who we feel is the best by who we personally relate to."

"You go boy!" Harmony joked in her Yankee voice.

"So with that being said, my first top five of all time Drumroll, please! But not in order is Tupac, Styles P, Jay-z, Nas, and Scarface... My second team of that era," I announced while taunting Top, " is DMX, Ice Cube, Bun B, Andre Three Stacks, and Kurupt! My sixth man on the first team would be Fat Pat. On the second team, it would be Jadakiss."

"Okay, Okay," Top mentioned, "Now we're getting somewhere! Nation I swear, it's like pulling teeth trying to get answers out of you!" I carried on while we all laughed, "Now my first team for this era and once again, not in order is… Rozay, Jeezy, Kendrick, T.I., and the late great Neighborhood Nipsey Hussle."

"Long Live Nipsey!" The General shouted as we all repeated in reverence. Nip had just passed on a few months prior and it was still fresh in the hearts of Hip Hop culture.

"Continuing on with my list, my second team is, The God A.Z., who just continues to get better to me over time. Lil Wayne because this nigga influence the game got everybody on this rockstar shit, plus dude nice with the mic. Fabolous and Nicki Minaj. That soul tape collection by Fabolous was legendary!"

"Nicki Minaj though!?" Top asked in astonishment.
"Yeah, nigga Nicki Minaj! That Mutha-fucka's super tough! Super flow!
"Yeah, Yeah, you're right. Top shot back, "I just wouldn't have never guessed she'd be on your list." That Hip Hop conversation continued all the way to L.A.

Niggas is Lucky (57) "If we buss out this shit"

      While in L.A. around two that morning, I took the Sprinter and cruised around Hollywood taking in all the sites and sounds. After driving for a minute, I ended up at a gas station on Sunset and Gower near 101 Hollywood Fwy. I pulled up to the gas pump and hopped out to pay. The store was closed, but there was a line outside, for people to pay at the window. I was the third person in line when something within me compelled me to turn around. You know how when you're watching a movie and the scene slows down so that you can feel the effect? That's how I felt when I saw those two Yukon Denalis pulled up on the side of the Sprinter bus.

      When I finally made it to the window to pay, the first Yukon's front window rolled down. I was able to see a silhouette of a dude as a succession of flashes came from whoever was taking photos. My heart skipped a beat, as I approached the homeless dude to give him the change I had left from paying for gas. My mind was reeling trying to decipher what the fuck I'd just seen. The homeless dude had been watching the whole play as well.

So once I handed him the change, he gestured towards the SUVs then said, "Ay, youngster I don't know what you got going on, but you better be careful." I nodded in response. I slowly walked back toward the Sprinter bus in a daze, not knowing what to expect. When my phone rang and I dug in my pocket to answer; the two Yukons sped off.

"Yo, my youth waa gwaan? Where you at?"

"I'm on Sunset right now getting gas." Harmony and I talked while I pumped the gas. In my mind, I was tripping from what I'd just witnessed. I said to myself, my mind couldn't have been playing tricks on me, because the homeless dude had seen it too. But I could never tell anyone about that episode.

On our third day in Dallas, we were at Denny's on Wheatland and Westmoreland, after performing at DG's. We were well into our meals, relaxing, taking in the atmosphere and conversing with each other. Admirers who noticed us, came to either take pictures or engage in small talk and or asked questions like:

"Nation, how you knew niggas would set it off in
Oak Cliff over Rodney Simmons?!"
"Top Star, what's popping blood!"
"Nation, you think niggas will ever unite?"

While chopping game with fans, a couple of dudes
walked by that caught my attention and made my heart
skip a beat. I caught my snap, gathered my composure,
and happened to glance at Harmony who was sitting
catty-corner from me reaching for her holster!

"Yo, gal lower that!" I pleaded while motioning
with my hand for her to calm down!

The next morning, I woke up early and got my
hygiene together then left the room. I walked outside
of the hotel to the right of the Hilton, where there was
a small man-made pond. I noticed the pond a few days
before but that morning I went because I was able to
watch the sunrise.

I stood by the bank of the pond, feeding last night's
leftovers to the fish, ducks and turtles. I got a text from
Harmony asking about my whereabouts. I texted back

my location. About fifteen minutes later, she appeared and walked over to me. She wrapped my right arm in her arms as I continued to feed the animals.

"Good morning, my King," she muttered seductively: I playfully mean-mugged her then responded,

"Yo, gal, what I told you bout that?!" We both laughed.
"But no seriously Nation, are you okay?"
"Yeah, I'm good baby, why you ask?"
"Mi seen you last night, mi seen the way you reacted when you saw them dudes."
"Oh, that was nothing."
"Nothing... Your heart skipped a beat." I turned to look into her eyes with a puzzled look and asked, "How would you know that?!"
"Because for some reason, mi a feel your heart skip a beat too."
"What!?" I responded perplexed and astounded as she continued.

"That's what made mi reach for mi tool. But that wasn't the first time that feeling came over mi. The first time mi felt that was at Jay's uncle's home when you met that old woman. Whatever she said or did, had you shook, but not a feeling of fear. It was a feeling of admiration. But the second time, when we were in L.A. the extreme feeling of fear came over mi."

"So that's why you called me that morning to see where I was at and what I was doing."

"Yea, that feeling of fear jolted mi out of mi sleep. Mi called to see if you were okay."

Wow, I thought to myself while we stood silently watching the sunrise. I thought about the incident that occurred last night as well as the one in L.A. One of the dudes at the Denny's resembled the silhouette of the man snapping the photos of the Sprinter bus. Although for some mysterious reason, Harmony was able to feel the fear and other emotions from those encounters, I didn't want to tell her why I had those feelings. Plus on top of that, I was trying to wrap my head around how she could feel what I felt anyway.

Walking down "Six street" in Austin TX after performing at the South by Southwest Festival, a gorgeous dark mocha-skinned female, with an angelic aura approached us. Once she got close, she approached me. Everyone stopped to try to get a feel for what was happening, while the woman and I stood face to face.

She raised her hand towards my face, then asked, "Nation, is it really you?" In a confused tone, I answered yes trying my best to understand where this was going. She surveyed the contents of my face with her fingers.

"It is you!" she smiled while tears began to develop. I was completely speechless when she asked, "You don't remember me, do you?"

I solemnly replied, "No I'm sorry, I don't."

"I'm Elizabeth, you came to visit me a while back. As she continued, I tried to make sense of all of this and remember anything she was saying. She carried on, "I had an acute degenerative eye disease, remember? I was blind." The events of my last night in prison came rushing back to me. That night King Aswad literally shocked my consciousness to another place.

"Ms. Elizabeth, is it? Is there anywhere we can go and talk?"

She grabbed my hand and pointed up the street. "There's a small cafe up the street."

We all took our seats at the table in the cafe. At that moment, Billie Holiday's Strange Fruit was playing at low volume. The low lighting gave the cafe the ambiance of a jazz lounge. Elizabeth formally introduced herself to the OmegaGuard, while we all looked at the menus.

"Listen, Ms. Elizabeth," she raised her hand to stop me mid-sentence.
"Please, everyone who knows me calls me Mimi."
"Okay Mimi, this is going to sound stupid crazy, but what you're saying was reality to you was a dream to me!"

"But you were really there! You never said your name, but I'll never forget that voice! A while back when I heard your music, I knew it was you! When I found out that you were going to perform here at South by Southwest, I had to come see you again to tell you, thank you."

"Thank me? Thank me for what? I didn't do anything!"

"But you did!" She pressed on as tears began rolling down her face. "I was blind remember?!"

"Yea I remember you having those bandages over your eyes."

"But do you remember what you told me?"

"No, I don't recall."

"I was about to touch your face but before you left abruptly, you placed a finger on each of the bandages on my eyes and said and I quote, See the future, for Aswanna okay! I initially thought you were a psychiatrist. But then you left so suddenly, I thought I had been dreaming. Until the next morning when I awoke and was able to see! To this day, no one can believe what happened, nor can doctors scientifically prove how, but I know how!"

All I could say was, "Wow!"

"Since then, I've graduated college, completed my thesis for The Black Nationalistic Ascension Codes, plus I'm in the process of completing my first book called "Hip Hop, The True Black Religion."

"Oh my God!" Top's crazy ass blurted out, "This chic's amazing!" Jay whistled in astonishment. She showed me a photo on her iPhone of her holding a little boy.

"I've also had a son whom I named after you." I glanced at Harmony to see her reaction.

Harmony looked back at me, smiled then gestured with both hands as if to say,"It is what it is." Mimi handed me her phone.

I stared at the picture for a second then asked, "How old is he?"

"He'll be two on September 13th."

I thought that was super crazy! We have the same birthday!

"Listen," I commanded as I handed her phone back.

"This is the last stop of our year-long promo tour. Tomorrow we're headed back to Houston. Put my number in your phone. Once I get settled in, I'll send for you and my godson, aight. You're officially family now. That's my word."

Down Time (58)

After spending over a year on tour, I was back in "Screwton" Tx. I took a few weeks off to breathe. I went and put a downpayment on a condo on the west side near Katy, TX. It was a beautiful two-story duck-off. Halfway through the tour after Chi-town, Tiara went back to Baltimore to be with her family. Her father had been diagnosed with stage cancer, so she wanted to be there for support. I was alone until Harmony came over. She lent a hand by helping me decorate the place. A few weeks after my new sister Mimi and God's son, Baby Nation came to visit. Whew! When I tell you baby Nation was all over the place! I loved it though, because everything started to resemble the life I had been aiming for. Mimi came out of the kitchen with two plates of food and sat them on the coffee table. She watched me play with Baby Nation for a moment and seemed to be in deep thought.

"Nation," she asserted, soliciting my attention.

I answered, "What's up?"

"There's something I want to talk to you about that's going to sound crazy."

"Crazy!?!" I shot back laughing."As if my life is normal. Talk to me, Mimi."

She thought for a second then continued, "I'm trying to figure out where to start."

"Just let it out, lady."

"Okay Nation, here it goes... Baby Nation is your child."

I looked at her and in a confused state asked, "Um, what are you talking about?"

"Nation, A few months after my fiancé passed away and my degenerative eye disease grew more aggressive, I started having these crazy dreams.

One night I had a dream, I was in a huge church. That's when I first saw your face. You put a ring on my finger." In a mesmerized state, I peered directly into her eyes and asked,

"You had a veil over your face!?"

"Yes," She shouted passionately, "So you remember what happened next right?!"

"Mimi, you mean to tell me that we were in each other's dreams!?"

"Yes, it seems that way, because that's the night I conceived Baby Nation. I counted the months back to that night."

At that point, I was at a loss for words. She continued, "Of course, I didn't bring that part up that night at the cafe, in front of everyone when I showed you the photo. Believe me Nation, I'm trying to figure this out, just like you are." I grabbed Baby Nation's bottle from the table, cradled him, and handed him the bottle. I looked up at Mimi and declared, "Whether we made love somewhere in some intergalactic realm or whatever, you and Baby Nation will forever be a part of this lion's pride."

Before Mimi had arrived we had already been brainstorming on the phone about creating a comprehensive community plan to address some of the issues young people face in urban communities. So when she arrived and we got past that intergalactic part, we picked up where we left off. We came up with a variety of ways that would resonate with the youth like having classes that tap into each individual's talents. Teaching them how to match their skills, talents and interests to careers that fit their traits. And also helping them develop an awareness of their strengths and weaknesses as they learn how to manage them. We planned to have a meeting at a place in South Park called the Shrine of the Black Madonna.

After being on vacation, I returned to the studio. Now it seemed the whole world knew who we were; the internet was going crazy over the way the events I rhymed about unfolded. Everybody was trying to interview and collaborate with me, which made me reclusive and a lil paranoid because I was also getting death threats. Top Star flew back down from Atlanta, to vibe with me and feature on a few of my songs. Within a month, I completed an album named "Grand Finale." I decided to release the album Juneteenth to commemorate the last slaves to be freed.

Tiara called to let me know she would be on the next flight to Houston that evening. Mimi, Baby Nation and I went to pick up Tiara from

Intercontinental Airport. Asia and Mimi had previously talked with each other on the phone about various things before formally meeting at the airport. They planned to get their hair done together, so I dropped them off at Peaches' hair salon. Afterwards, I drove back to my spot to get a USB chip I forgot that had some tracks on it I wanted to vibe to. On my way there my phone rang.

"Yo lion, waa gwaan? Where you at?" Harmony asked, a lil more serious than usual.

"Shit," I answered, "I'm on my way to my spot, what's up?"

"Yo, you not have no tool on you?"

"Naw, why?"

She sucked her teeth then responded, "Yo what kind of foolishness you got going on? You not carrying no tool?!"

"Wait a minute Harmony, why you asking me about that kind of shit anyway, what's the problem?"

"Cause mi feeling leery, mi vexed. Something not sit well with me. Look mi a come link up with you."

"Listen gal, I'm okay. I got heat at my spot and you know I know how to use them. So don't worry baby, I'll be aight."

"Bless lion."

I hung up the phone with her as I pulled into the driveway of my condo. Not even five minutes later, I got a call from Tiara. I first ignored the call because I knew Harmony had called her. She called again as I stepped into my condo.

I answered, "Hey, lady."
"Where are you and what are you doing Nation?"
"Now don't do that. I told you what I was going to do before I left you at Peaches."
"So have you made it?"
"Yes parole officer," I replied joking. "I just walked in the door."

"How long do you plan on being there?"

"I don't know. I was going to put a meal together, grab my USB chip, and make my way back to you."

"Well, you need to hurry up, mister."

"Okay, lady damn! Calm down!"

Grand Finale (59)

I stayed on the phone with Asia the whole time I was home. The moment I walked out the door towards my car, Harmony called again while I was talking to Asia. I texted Harmony and told her that I was on the phone with Asia. Harmony texted back saying she was on her way and was already close. Well, those of you who read the beginning of this story, you know what happened next.

For those who want to know who assassinated me, it was Rebel. Some years after he escaped from us, The Feds swooped down on him with a host of charges that got him a thousand years figuratively speaking. The Feds and the CIA were the ones who had been following me snapping photos. Sometime during his sentence, those agencies concluded that I was the long-awaited Prophet of Aswanni Prophecy. By them finding out that Rebel and I had a past, they gave him an option which he gladly obliged. The day I got hit, Harmony had been having premonitions which is why she was calling and asking me if I had my tool. She arrived a few seconds too late, although she was able to avenge my death.

Once it hit the news that I had been killed it sent shockwaves throughout the country. Seven days later, The Grand Finale was released on Juneteenth as scheduled. Within the week The Grand Finale went platinum. On the song called "The PayCheck," these bars set off riots and protests throughout the country:

"The one who shot me was sent by the government
    cause they knew, I was the one that would run it
up..."

The Sacred Commander (60) September 13th, 1996

The one who had supposedly been assassinated in Las Vegas was escorted out of the country to Puerto Rico. Nuns, nurses, and surgeons waited for the plane to land to rush him to the sanctuary. The sanctuary had a state-of-the-art medical facility within it where they operated on him several times. He had been shot multiple times in vital areas which made his injuries near fatal. It took months of rehabilitation and therapy to bring him back to optimal health. With renewed vigor, he went back to military training, while he made preparations to meet the masters of The Esoteric Art of Rhythm-Mystic Poetry:

The Ancient Order of Apex Omega (61) Location: Ancient Ethiopia 1578 B.C.

An ancient mystical mystery system was created at the sixth cataract of the Blue Nile in Ethiopia. The Order Of Apex Omega was in the process of initiating the first Pure Hearted soul to Supreme Stewardship. During the ceremony, a spectacular spectacle appeared in the sky. Unidentified flying objects staged a dramatic display in the sky as if to confirm and celebrate their satisfaction and endorsement of the newly appointed Supreme Steward.

The primary responsibility of the newly formed position of the Supreme Steward was threefold; which was to spiritually, politically, and economically create balance throughout the kingdom of Ethiopia/Kush and Egypt/Kemet. On that day the extraterrestrials, who were then considered to be "Gods" had something far greater in mind.

One of the space crafts descended and landed near the Nile. The commanders of the craft telepathically contacted the Supreme Steward and invited him and a few of his brethren to meet with them. They all boarded the spacecraft. Moments later, the craft shot off to space. Twenty-one days later they returned accompanied by the commanders of the spacecraft. Legend has it that during his time in space, The Supreme Steward was taught the "ways of heaven." There, standing on the bank of the Blue Nile, "the order" witnessed the Steward being baptized by the Gods.

As the Steward arose from out of the Nile, his ailing features shockingly began to reverse. Within minutes, he looked as though he was in his early twenties. By being pure of heart and taught the ways of heaven, the Steward was granted the power by the Gods to become the first catalyst after being baptized. It activated the Nile's healing and youth regenerative power. The power only lasts as long as the Steward is alive. The first of the Supreme Stewards lived for two hundred forty years before he was killed. Once the Steward passes on, the healing, youthful regenerative power ceases until a new intergalactic cycle begins and a new pure-hearted soul is born. Only the highest of the order of Apex Omegas who are the keepers of the knowledge know where the waters with regenerative elixir would be found next.

Ancient Scrolls Recovered (62)

In the year 1571 A.D. Buddhist Monks who were in Aswanna during the time of the "Fall" were able to flee the impending invasion. They were able to carry the ancient scrolls which were written on papyrus, millennia before by scribes in Nubia. But the scrolls were lost in Tibet when the temple was destroyed by a great earthquake.

During the time of the American Civil War, monks in Tibet recovered the scrolls that possessed the oracles of the ancient form of Hip Hop and described the African-American slaves as the bearers of the art of Rhythm-Mystic Poetry. The text also described that during the eve of the new millennia, the so-called fabled fountain of healing and youth would be found in Aswanna.

The Word Is Born (63) 1996

The reason for the Commander's renewed vigilance was due to those attempts on his life and events that took place throughout the world verified the authenticity of the ancient texts. On his untraceable mobile phone, he contacted one of his comrades in New York City.

"What's up my nigga!"
"You're alive?!"
"Hell Yeah, they shot me all of those times, but real niggas don't die! Just like the scrolls foretold. Now it's time to get the next phase popping because the Omega prophet has been born."
His comrade proclaimed, "Word is Born!"

Although no one knew who the prophet would be or where he would emerge; the Commander appointed messengers on each coast throughout the United States as well as on the islands. Their duty was to distribute "game" through the ethereal channels of hip-hop to whomever would rise to be the prophet.

Alliances (64)

The Sacred Commander traveled to Cuba to connect with his aunt who was a college professor. She was well-connected with heads of state, military officials, and religious leaders throughout the globe. When he walked into his aunt's home, he noticed the painting on the wall. It was a painting of the Madonna and Child which depicted him and his mother as the black version of Mary and Jesus.

"Auntie you gotta be kidding me?" He asked while smiling, as he hugged her.
"They have their Jesus, I have mine," she countered. She lived in the same compound as Fidel Castro, so she was protected by the Cuban military.

"You were just a child the last time I saw you face to face. Back in the early seventies, we received the ancient manuscripts that contained the texts referring to the art of Rhythm-Mystic Poetry. Those who studied the scrolls and knew of your birth, celebrated it because it signified the eve of the age of the "Devoted

Pure Hearted Ones." She waved for him to follow her as she moved towards the backyard.

"But as the prophecy states, the Alpha Child has to be cultivated and play his part. That's what pushes prophecy forward. You also have to prepare for the Omega Child." They stood for a moment as they watched the kids play soccer.

She asked, "So considering the circumstances, how do you feel?"

"I'm okay, I guess. I'm just stressed because I haven't been able to talk to my mother or sister."

"I know exactly how you feel. When I fled from the belly of the beast, years passed before I was able to contact my daughter. You just stay strong and continue the work of liberation. So my next question is, where do you go from here? What do you have planned?"

He looked out at the kids playing soccer, while he took time to reflect on his answer.

"I plan to meet with the keepers of the order."

"I believe that would be your best move."

The soccer ball rolled toward them, she scooped the ball up and threw it back to the kids.

"I also believe you should make your presence felt amongst those who are in high places. Those members of those various orders who believe and have faith in you need to see you. They are your allies. They need to know that the work they've done has not been in vain."

He sighed heavily and stood in silence for a moment.

"Yeah, I know... But I want you to come with me."

The first place his auntie took him was Vatican City, Rome. Stepping into the Cathedral, there were people scattered about praying, reading, and talking amongst themselves. They were later confirmed to be members of a coalition of "Orders."The most prominent is the "Opus Deit" which in Latin means "Work of God."

Word was that the Sacred Commander would be making an appearance there, so that was the reason for a lot of people from many sects of "Orders" in attendance. Once the members noticed his aunt, his disguise was insignificant because it was already known whom she'd be traveling with.

At that time, she had been one of the FBI's most wanted, which made her travel inconspicuously throughout the years. She'd become a pro at maneuvering undetected, many times with the assistance of various "Orders."

The Commander continued to follow his aunt up the middle row of the aisle to go meet with the Pope who was in his office awaiting their arrival. Members began to surround him, bowing and chanting various attributes associated with what he represented.
"The Shining Serpent, thankful to God!"
A few shouted in unison.
"Sagrado Comandante!..."Son of Madonna!...Amaru!".

Although he understood why he was being venerated, it made him uncomfortable. The crowd was stopped abruptly by the bishop, who'd come from the office area beside the altar.

"Make way for them!" He shouted twice making sure the crowd heard him. They did as directed and dispersed allowing the Commander and his aunt to continue on their path.

The bishop stood waiting for them to reach him. Once he greeted them, he gestured for them to follow him to the pope's office. Pope John Paul rose from his chair to greet the Commander's aunt whom he'd known for years. When she first fled the "Belly" of the beast, over those trumped-up murder charges, Pope John Paul reached out to her. From then on a bond had been created. They would periodically meet, exchange information concerning human rights, and report to each other any event that occurred in relation to the "Rhythm-Mystic Prophecies."

Pope John embraced her, and kissed her on both cheeks then announced, "My little dragon slayer!" Which was the moniker he'd given her since the first time they'd met.

"How are you doing, John?" She asked.
"Just grateful to be alive and of assistance, during these fantastic times!"

"And these are fantastic times indeed," she acknowledged while taking a seat across from the Pope's desk. Pope John turned towards the commander. "Amaru, the Sacred Commander. It's an honor to finally meet you." They shook hands and took seats across from each other.

Pope John Paul continued, "Amaru, when your mother's water broke and she went into contractions, the Earth began to slow down! When she went into labor with you that fateful summer day at 7:47 pm, the Earth stopped spinning for seven hours! The world went crazy until around 2:30 am when the sun finally began to set, during the time she gave birth to you. Later that night, Unidentified flying objects swarmed the area in Ethiopia where the first "Supreme Steward" had been baptized.

Those of us who are members of this "Coalition of Orders" knew what those events meant. But the "others" whom we've coined as "Slumberers," which are the masses of people across the world, were horrified. We celebrated your birth, the birth of the Alpha Child; the one who is destined to ascend the throne and make way for the Omega Child, The Buddha, The Prophet, The Supreme Steward once the time comes."

"John," His auntie asserted, "We need clearance to continue on this "Tour of Duty" to forge much-needed alliances."

"Yes, you're right," Pope John agreed.

The cardinal in attendance reached into a file cabinet and pulled out a file. He handed it to Pope John who took out two sheets of paper. The cardinal made a call and handed it to Pope John.

"Yes, we're going to need universal clearances for two."

He hung up the phone, signed his signature on those papers, and stamped the Vatican's seal of approval on them.

He handed one to each of them. "No government agency, the world over, is allowed to detain you. But be aware of that rogue element within the United States Government that seeks to stop you at any cost. And above all else, don't expose yourselves to the public. Have a safe journey dragon slayer! Take care of him!" he insisted as he smiled.

The next place they flew to on their tour was to meet Vladimir Putin in Russia at the Kremlin. Speaking with Putin, the Commander hoped he wouldn't have to go this far, when it came time in order to truly free his people.

"I will see to it that Russia is of service to you when the time comes. I hate those fucking Americans anyway. Always meddling in our affairs as if their hands are clean." The Commander could feel the animosity that stirred within Putin as he spoke about America. Putin wanted to crush America.

The Commander didn't hate America, what he wanted was what he knew "She" was capable of, which was distributing that inheritance to the descendants of the slaves that she had promised to pay. That bill for services rendered was now in the trillions.

From Russia, they traveled to Japan, China, India, Saudi Arabia, Israel, Ethiopia, Germany and Great Britain. All of whom pledged their allegiance to the Commander.

The Omega Guard (65)"Lost in a whirlwind, like Garvey; Resurrect the movement, Omega Guard Team" 2022 A.D.

By the New Year, "The Grand Finale" went diamond. The Omega Guard pressed on doing shows, speaking at colleges, political forums, and so forth. America got spooked when bars from the song came to life called "Falling."

"Hurricanes in Cali, great quakes in Boston
were just the beginning of America's sorrow
This paradigm shift hurts her to the core
like when asteroids hit Mt Rushmore"...

This song sent people to search for answers in their respective religions. America seemed to be being judged for its sheer negligence and callous approach to dealing with mother Africa's offspring. The song called "PayCheck" which according to news reports brought out Conservatives and right-wing militia groups calling to boycott, denounce and protest the song, the chorus went:

"Talk that shit, rep that shit!
My ancestors built this bitch!
Now it's time ya'll pay that check!
Pay that check! Pay that check!"

Top Star who picked up where I left off released a mixtape called, "Each Nigga On Every Street" the first single was called "Tupac's Eyes" and swept through hoods which such force that it ignited a fire in the streets with bars like:

"I'm looking through the world,
with Tupac's eyes,
I did a "seance" then made Tupac rise!"

Harmony, who normally wouldn't involve herself with the music, decided to speak poetry on a few songs. She also chanted in the ancient Aswannan tongue, it was epic. On the other hand, Harmony, having military training experience, along with Top Star becoming a five General of the Blood Gang, came up with the idea to go to as many urban neighborhoods throughout the country as possible.

The objective was for Top Star to galvanize as many street kings of their respective gangs as the Crips, Bloods, G.D.s, and Vice Lords. Harmony and other military vets could teach self-defense and military training to the urban youth. Jay the General linked up with Robert "Supreme" Economic Johnson and held basic financial literacy and group economic courses.

The whole movement they were creating had that 1960s Panther vibe to it. Jay unveiled the Omega Guard flag to the team. It was the black and gold 12-pointed star cross he showed me at the "Pure Heart" video shoot. To the right of the star, he added black and gold stripes similar to the United States flag. The Omega Guard distributed the flag to every urban neighborhood. Soon after the flags started popping up everywhere Blacks and whoever else pledged their allegiance lived.

Eighteen months had passed since the release of "The Grand Finale." Tiara had given birth to an eight-and-a-half-pound baby boy, Omega. Omega was now close to nine months. She was sitting in a hospital room with little Omega in her lap watching the world news. She raised little Omega in the air towards the T.V.

"See boy, look what your daddy started."

The person she was sitting next to lying in bed, emerged from his slumber and uttered, "Who did what?" Tiara turned to the right and screamed with joy,

"Nation! You're awake! I knew you would wake up, I never gave up on you!"
As I tried to gather myself I asked, "How long have I been gone?"

"You've been in a coma for over a year and a half!" She raised little Omega up to show me.
"This is Omega, your son!"

I rose up a little to look at him, even though I was still too weak to hold him.
"Wow," I expressed in wonder as I looked at him.

Words couldn't describe how I felt gazing into the eyes of this mini version of myself. I stared in amazement, as he bounced his bobblehead around smiling without a care in the world. Our eyes locked and he looked at me as to say, "Nigga, where have you been?"

The moment was interrupted when doctors and nurses rushed in to check on me. They checked all of my vital signs and asked how I felt. After confirming that my vital signs were stable they left. Tiara and I returned to our moment.

I felt strong enough so I asked, "Let me hold him okay?" She handed him to me. When I grabbed and held him our eyes locked again. His facial expressions gave me the impression that he was peering through my soul. I had to break free from the spell of his gaze to resume the conversation with Tiara.

While I played with Omega I asked, "Asia, what did you mean when you told Omega, to look and see what your daddy started?"

"Boy, you've been in a coma for eighteen months! A lot has happened! Jay still released your album "The Grand Finale" on Juneteenth, a week after you went into the coma. Since then, that album has sold thirty million globally!"

"Three times diamond!?" I asked, astonished.

"Yes, the things you talked about and prophesied, set off a tidal wave of events that sent the country into chaos! People are marching, rallying, rioting, it's all crazy!"

"Wow! That's super wild!"

"Yea! And add that to the fact that Jay's uncle Benjamin became President of the United States!"

"What! Are you serious!?"

"Boy, I sang The Black National Anthem at the inauguration!"

The Speech (66) "I'm Amazing"
Standing on the podium, I'm trying to watch my sodium...

When Benjamin heard about what happened, he decided to hide me in a hospital near D.C. for my safety. After finding out I had emerged from the coma, he sent a brigade of secret servicemen to retrieve me. While on the way to his house, Benjamin scheduled an emergency press conference on the White House lawn.

I pulled up with a motorcade of Lincoln limos. I was helped out of the limo by secret servicemen because I was still weak from the coma. I needed a cane to support me as I walked towards the White House lawn. It seemed like every major news network and journalist on the planet was there. Once the media circus noticed us, cameras began flashing. No one knew who I was, because I had on a hoodie and dark shades. I was guided to the stage and watched as the Secretary-General spoke.

"This press conference has been called because of striking new revelations that have been revealed to us. Here to convey this information to us." I was assisted to the podium, as he introduced me.

"Nation Omega Lord."

Once I reached the podium, I took my hoodie off and the media went berserk! You could hear the gasp from the media in unison as cameras flashed.

"First and foremost I liked to give thanks and praise to my ancestors. Although they went through the unthinkable, they were still able to leave a long-lasting legacy of strength, resilience, and perseverance despite being notoriously oppressed throughout centuries.

Everything that could be done was done over a span of decades to derail the prophet from arising, once Hip-Hop rebirthed in its present form. Not knowing who he would be nor where he would emerge, the government went on a campaign to destroy black communities, by flooding communities with drugs, deadly diseases, and guns among other things. All while systematically incarcerating Black men at alarming rates.

The deliberate disenfranchisement, marginalization, and systematic oppression have reached its zenith. The economic disparities are at the crux of the matter. Our people need to be compensated for the work our ancestors did for centuries forcibly to make this country what it is today. That's our inheritance that is being withheld from us. If our ancestors had been compensated during Emancipation as promised, there wouldn't be such grave disparities between the two races. We've had enough of the deliberate stalling and neglect that has been perpetuated by the United States Government.

While I was unconscious in a coma, My ancestors came to me and revealed to me the location of my people's capital, had it been finished during their time. So in the coming weeks, we are going to embark on a journey to find evidence of the mystical, Aswanna homeland."

Weeks before we embarked on that journey, I had to go to recover one of my Omega Guard family members. In my absence, Top Star has lost himself in the chaos, and became what I'd initially felt would happen to me. In the shadow of the night, Harmony and I, accompanied by secret servicemen, who would for now be our official bodyguards took a G3 flight down to Miami to bring my bro "home" figuratively speaking.

My sources told me that he would be at the "King of Diamonds" strip joint. At King of Diamonds, I had to call D.C. and tell Homeland Security to tell these secret service muthafuckas to back off. We wanted to go incognito, not sticking out like a sore thumb. After that silly shit got cleared up, Harmony and I stepped into the place. I held her hand as she led the way. You'd swear she's been here before by the way she maneuvered through the place. She guided us to the V.I.P section where there was this huge ass dude standing in front of the rope, built like Bobby fucking Lashley! She whispered something in his ear which made him take a step back, look at her then me. A second later, he unlatched the rope, stepped aside, and let us through.

Later I asked her, what did she tell "Bobby Lashley" to make him let us in V.I.P.? She grabbed my 12-point star cross ring on my finger and then humorously countered, "It's the jewelry, stupid! "Only the Omega Guard, Top, mi, you, and tha General have them emblem there plus mi told him who we were, but we wanted to keep a low profile." Till this day, I don't know if she was lying but whatever she told him worked.

I was glad that up until that moment, no one noticed me. I had on a black fitted hoodie, black fitted cap, black locs, glasses on some big homie Trae-Tha-Truth shit. I didn't want to be noticed; I didn't want all that attention from the fucking press conference on the White House lawn that I was sure the whole world has seen.

She spotted Top Star, who was surrounded by Haitian niggas and strippers. There were five gold bottles sitting on the table and he also had one in his hand. When I saw him, he reminded me of how my state of mind was after Savage got killed.

I was on some self-destructive don't give a fuck about life shit, smoking "sherms", popping pills, and sipping drank. As we approached him, he noticed Harmony, then me walking hand and hand with her. His eyes lit up with excitement, looking as though he was about to announce that I was there. I raised one finger to my mouth signifying for him to chill and not say anything. I gestured for him to come with us. He rose up and told his team something then followed us outside to the parking lot.

We embraced as tears fell from his eyes.

"Nation! I saw that shit with you at the White House! Man, I thought you'd never come out of that coma!"

To lighten up the moment, while expressing how I felt about the whole ordeal in my Jeezy voice, I growled,

"I'm Amazing! Yeah, I'm all that!"

We laughed that off for a moment, then I got down to the reason I was there. "Top, I got word from up top," I said while using my first two fingers on each hand to signify quotation marks.

"That you got these Haitians down here taking out white folks on some hateful shit." He lowered his head but didn't respond. I put my arm around him and continued, "Bro you know we don't rock like that."

"This ain't the 1700s, you're not Toussaint L'Ouverture, and this ain't Haiti's baby. Believe me, I know exactly how you feel but you can't let hate consume you. You hate the system, not the people. Most white folks today are nothing like the people who created this fucked up system. Most feel the same way we do about what's going on. Top you're a leader, remember we're in it, to spit it like Nas said. Spitting the highest truth, not the lie-st truth. I already made your bond, so come on home...Let's finish what we started. I promise it's going to be legendary."

Aswanna Africa (67)

I swear it was every major news network in the world following me and the Omega Guard, in a motorcade of Land Rovers and Hummers while helicopters hovered. We were in the first vehicle while a guide drove us. We reached a particular area and something in my spirit began to stir. "Hey, stop right here!" I shouted, looking out at the terrain. As soon as he pulled over, I hopped out and began walking allowing the spirit to guide me. This area was a beautiful stretch of land. There were all kinds of animals roaming the area. I walked about a hundred fifty yards as my team and a host of government officials, media reporters and secret servicemen followed behind.

I knelt on the sand, grabbed a handful of it and kissed it as it flowed through my fingers. I then was compelled to draw a sign of what looked like a 12-

pointed star inside the sand as I said a silent prayer. While I said my prayer, a solitary tear dropped from my eye onto the sign I'd drawn.

All of a sudden, the sand on the ground began shifting and shaking; something was rising up out of the ground. As it continued to rise, we all had to pedal backwards. Once we realized what was rising up from the ground, we all were astonished! It was a fully erected gold and pearl castle!

I continued to let the spirit guide me as I stepped into the castle. Everyone took a cue from me and followed me. The spirit led me to the treasure room and when I stepped in I saw jewels everywhere! Sitting against the wall in the back of the room was a gigantic treasure chest. It was filled to the brim with jewels and on top was a crown. I stepped over all the jewels that were scattered about in the room to get to the crown. Reaching the treasure chest, I picked up the crown and put it on my head.

I looked at the crowd and roared, "It's time that my people return home!" Everyone gasped in amazement;

the whole world was shook to its core! They had witnessed prophecy be fulfilled! Aswanni people the world over, who were able to, could finally make their trek to their ancestral homeland.

Meditation (68)

The "Sacred Commander" was in a Tibetan temple when he received word concerning the prophet. He had resided there for well over a decade after that "call of duty" tour with his aunt. There he studied, trained and became one of the highest masters of the "Esoteric Art Of Rhythm-Mystic Poetry."

He listened as the Buddhist monk relayed the message to him while he was in the midst of meditating. "Master, the prophet has arrived in the ancient land of Aswanna! He has also resurrected the castle, just as the scrolls foretold!"

"Yeah, it's done!" The Commander proclaimed. "The time is near, The Kingdom shall rise!" Arising from his meditative pose," he continued, "Now let's hope that we won't have to take it there."

Smile For Me (69) "For the next generation"

On the flight back to the United States, I passed the time on Air Force One, watching Scarface of the Ghetto Boys, solo and group videos. I thought about my grandpa Boo-Bee, and how he'd bring me Hip-Hop music, which at the time was considered to be way beyond my age bracket. But I still remembered what he'd told me when he gave me that "Untouchable" CD.

"Look here, Nation. A lot of this music you're not going to understand until you get older. The reason I'm passing these jewels to you now is for when you're mature enough, you can refer back to these musical scriptures and view life with more clarity."

Watching "Mind Playing Tricks on Me," "Now I Feel You," "Till I Seen a Man Die," "Gangstas Don't Live That Long," as well as other classics, really had me reminiscing about my grandfather. I felt some type of way when the "Smile" video came on. Although I had seen this video a gazillion times, I got chills and the hairs on my neck stood up! I smiled as I looked out of the window at the sun while the song played on my Dre-beats earbuds.

There were two scenes in that video that had the most profound effect on that day. The first was of a child who watched as the depiction of Tupac hanging on a makeshift cross came down from the cross and began his verse. The second was of the two Black men on the small boat at sea fighting each other.

After experiencing that surreal moment, I watched a few more videos before dozing off to sleep. I fell into a deep sleep and had a dream so vivid, I swore it was real. In that vision, I was in what looked like a Buddhist temple. In the rotunda, there were twelve monks that circled around the one who was levitating Indian style. I was compelled to approach the one within the circle slowly. A familiar voice began to speak to me telepathically.

"Hey lil bro, you've made it."
Uncertain about how to respond,
I replied, "Yeah, I guess."

The monk continued, "Since you're here, that means time draws near, so when you need me, I'll be there."
"Be where?" I asked.
"You'll know when you're at the fork in the road." I thought for a second about what he'd said, but since I couldn't wrap my head around his answer, I dismissed it, then asked, "Who are you?"

And just as he was about to remove the hood of his cloak from his head and reveal himself, I was awakened by Asia. She was sitting to the left of me. She nudged me to let me know that we had arrived in D.C. Coincidentally she was humming "Smile for me" to Omega.

"Advocates for that check" (70)

Back in D.C. we linked back up with President Sutton. I assisted and learned more about the procedures that went on the floor of the three branches of the government. Civil Rights activist groups like "The Black Congressional Caucus" as well as other forms of lawmakers all presented drafted bills to Congress. It's an effort to initiate the process of economic reconciliation which had been deliberately stalled by racists for well over a century.

When I found out the motto for what the "Black Congressional Caucus" used, I was blown away.

Their motto states:

"No permanent friends, no permanent enemies, just permanent interests."

The impression I got from it was "If neither party has our best interests in mind, we're not riding with either."

Me and the O.G. "Original God" Robert "Supreme Economics" Johnson fell in the Capital every day to watch, soak up and transfer "game." I had plugged in with his parole officer in Texas, before inviting him up. I could feel the tension in the air in the rotunda, from those that opposed everything that I stood for. They knew I was the reason for this surge of Advocacy for reparations and they hated it. The looks I got from some of the politicians from both sides were worth a thousand words. A Senator from Arkansas actually had the audacity to try to swing on me! Walking down the gallery with Eco during a temporary recess, this ole muthafucka tries to steal off on me! I just happened to catch him from the corner of my eye. I weaved his punch, then Eco grabbed his ass and put him in a sleeper hold until police officers arrived. Shit was just super crazy!

Once it came to be known to the world that bills were being presented to Congress and were seriously being considered, you should've seen the reaction! So-called Right-wing conservatives went ballistic; they didn't even want to apologize for slavery let alone talk about reparations. Their masks were coming off and the racist couldn't conceal their hate anymore. I watched it on the floor of the Senate chambers, the Supreme Court and the media.

The Exodus Tour (71)

Meanwhile, the Omega Guard assembled a tour that we labeled the "Exodus Tour." The tour was created to fund those who were not only the descendants of the Aswanni but also the descendants of slaves who wanted to make their exodus to their ancestral land. There were Hip Hop artists, Reggae, Afrobeats, Rock, Pop and Country. The last concert of the tour was in Aswanna in front of the castle. It seemed as though there were fans as far as the eye could see! Huge projector screens were put up every few yards so that fans could see the show. It was monumental! Our cue to start our performance was when the sun began to set. Tiara Sky opened up with the band playing, "Pure Hearted."

When she approached and mounted the stage, the band transitioned to the remake we'd put together of Whitley Houston's "I Have Nothing." She angelically began...

"Don't make me close one more door!
I don't really want to hurt anymore"...

During the last note, the center of the stage opens up. Top Star, The General, Harmony, and I, rose up from the stage on a platform. I was sitting on the actual throne of King Aswad, holding a golden staff in my left hand. Harmony stood directly to my right. Jay and Top stood on opposite sides of the throne. Once we were fully leveled with the stage, I stood revealing the three long gold chains around my neck. They were like the chains that dangled the medallions, down toward the bellies of the rappers at the beginning of the millennia. The first medallion was the Omega Guard star cross, the second was a golden Buddha and the third was of Tupac on the cross from the Makaveli album. I wore it because to me it signified the modern-day crucifixion of the black race.

On each of my arms, I had solid gold bracelets that went from my elbow to my wrists. On top of each one, there was the Omega Guard's insignia. I tapped the staff on the ground three times, which signaled fifty male and female soldiers, twenty-five on each side of the throne.

They were all wearing Star Trek military-style uniforms in Omega Guard colors. I thrusted the staff in the air, signaling for the troops to "about face" towards the crowd and salute them.

At the sametime, seven Jet fighters flew over. I lowered the staff and took the attachment from the top of it; which was a golden microphone. Harmony took the royal robe off me and as I handed her the staff she took a seat on the throne. All of this happened in a matter of minutes. During the interlude, Tiara hummed beautifully. She returned to the verse after the chorus. Afterwards, I began my verse with something like this:

"I shouldn't be alive, but I'm living it,
Grateful to those that are able to be witnesses,
I sat in a dark place in those prison cells,
Similar to the black race, going through living hell,
Now we stand on the shoulders of giants,

We gone show the world how to take down tyrants,
Tried to take me down, yea they thought I was
buried,
But the sun still rose, it was so legendary,
I rotate on my pivot foot, like Olajuwon,
Never underestimate, the heart of a champion,
This is the day, you can say, our ancestors made,
So why not be the ones, to finish the race,
Young leaders,
The only way they could beat us is to cheat us,
Until we start upping sticks and turn the heat up,
These are the thoughts of a soldier
With a golden heart,
I'll be the same, till death do us part,
Real talk!"…

Civil Race War (72)

Back in the United States, a full-fledged race war
had officially begun. One of the many white
supremacist groups went into a black middle-class

neighborhood in Jackson, Mississippi, and mowed it down slaughtering everyone. It was horrific. It was the worst terrorist attack on American soil. Worst than the Tulsa Race riots and 911 combined.

Shit was getting heavier by the second. Harmony told me that was why her and Top Star decided to train urban "Black" neighborhoods in self-defense and military drills to defend themselves. Her foresight was impeccable. She told me that the old saying still rang true which was "If you want peace, prepare for war." So with the assistance of some military veterans, they fortified the streets. Nothing like what happened in Jackson, happened anywhere our flag was raised.

Most of the country was outraged. They couldn't believe this senseless act of terrorism could've happened in America in this day and age. People from every race warred against these white supremacists. President Sutton declared martial law and tried to quell the unrest. He was unable to do much, lines had been drawn and lines had been crossed. The people could only take so much. Adding that to the fact that covertly politicians, lawmakers, and military officials had split and chosen sides.

I was sitting on the couch on the west wing of the White House upset and distraught over what I'd seen on television. Not wanting to be surrounded by the media and their cameras, I appeared on Instagram Live with tears flowing.

"It's been over a century and a half and they are still stalling us out of our inheritance! Had they paid our ancestors during the Emancipation as promised, we'd have our economic structure and base right now. It's so disrespectful to say the descendants of slaves shouldn't receive compensation because the repercussions of not doing so are still being felt to this very day! Now you're seeing an upheaval because niggas are fed up! It amazes me how America, the country that's supposed to be the guiding light of freedom and equality, has denied those same rights to its own citizens! We now see the true nature of this beast. The wool has been pulled off this wolf in sheep's clothing!"

Invasion (73)

Later that night, I fell asleep in the west wing. King Aswad appeared to me in my dreams.

"Aswad, I've done all I can do. I'm exhausted and I don't know where else to turn. I don't know what to do, It seems my words have fallen on deaf ears."

"You've done well," King Aswad complimented, "Take heart be not troubled. For the kingdom shall rise!..

"I hear you king, but the hate is real."

"Be patient, my son."

Moments later, I awoke to Secret servicemen scrambling to grab President Sutton, his family, his cabinet, and the rest of us to a safe place. There was a loud BOOM! Then a loud succession of rapid gunfire. Secret service officers were attempting to lead us to an underground bunker, but none of the electronics would work. So we all somehow ended up in the Oval Office.

By how loud the gunfire echoed, you could tell that whoever Secret Service officers were engaged in the gun battle were advancing. Just as I was about to tell

President Sutton to get my team some type of protection, I heard a familiar voice yell,

"Nation, tell President Sutton to surrender for the benefit of everyone!"

I initially thought that everyone heard it. "Benjamin!"

I yelled, "Did you hear him?!"

"Hear what?!" Sutton yelled back frantically. The voice yelled the same command again. I realized that the voice was telepathically speaking to me. My thoughts instantly went to what the Buddhist in my dream said about the fork in the road. I yelled at Sutton again, "Tell your officers to stand down!"

He looked terrified as he replied, "Are you out of your mind!"

"I can't explain it now, but believe me, just do it!"

The six Secret Service officers had their weapons aimed at the door, bracing themselves to engage. President Sutton, putting the fate of everyone in the room at my request, yelled to the officers,

"Stand down!" I repeat, stand down!" The lead officer reluctantly relayed the command into his earpiece, as the gunfight continued with whoever was invading the White House. The same officer who'd relayed the command earlier responded, "Yes, I'm serious! The President ordered us to stand down!" Within that moment, the gunfire ceased.

We all were trapped like rats in a cage. Whoever these insurgents were came through the door. They had beams pointed at all of us as the last soldier walked in. The soldiers parted as he stepped from between them and towards me. At that point, I ain't gone lie, I thought I was finished! When he reached me, he raised his night vision goggles, so I could see his face. He then saluted me! When it registered in my mind who it was I was shocked! I wouldn't have believed it had I not seen him!

Victory Aswanna (74) 2045 A.D

It's the year 2045, and I'm 49 years old. I'm hanging out at the castle which is now a museum in Victory Aswanna that is named after my daughter. I'm on my way to Omega Guard Central, which is the city part of Victory. There, I'm going to meet up with my family to go to the annual Aswanna Ascension festival. This is the day we commemorate our ancestors, as well as Aswanna's resurrection and subsequent rise onto the world stage.

There, I will meet up with my mother, the Omega guard and all my children. My youngest, who are girls from Harmony, are named Victory and Essence. Omega, my oldest "biological son" heir to the throne, is taking up law at Apex College, where my Godson Lil' Nation just graduated after double majoring in neuroscience and if I'm not mistaken software engineering. Dude's a technological genius. His mother Elizabeth Scott and Stephen "Top Star" Gaines are professors there. Apex College is located in Aswanna's capital which is named Essence. I named my youngest daughter after the capital. Jason "The General" Miller, jet sets across the globe on behalf of Aswanna, making diplomatic moves. Robert "Supreme Eco" Johnson, is my chief economic adviser.

The population of Aswanna is close to 9 million. Most Blacks stayed in America, after receiving the southern states. Aswanna's cities, towns and villages are thriving beautifully. Our main sources of energy are solar and wind power. Most of us are either vegan and or vegetarian unless it's seafood. Shut up, Harmony!

Hip Hop's Aswanna's official religion, thanks to Elizabeth. Our economy primarily thrives on Hip Hop tourism, technology, manufacturing, and green energy which is where most of us invested the money we received from reparations. Along with the influx of adherents who make their annual pilgrimage to the "Ascension Festival! Millions of people from across the world come here for the Hip Hop Global-7-13 Summit. The way that people the world over are converting to the religion of Hip Hop, Aswanna will soon be the religious capital of the world! Plus by me being around for at least another two hundred years, (Yeah, I said two hundred!) The plan is to make Ethiopia one of the global economic capitals of the world while also changing the name to New Eden. Hence in essence fulfilling the prophecy of making Africa a Global power.

I bet y'all dying to know what happened all those years ago at the White House! The reason the electricity wasn't working was because of the EMP, Electromagnetic Pulse, that insurgents used to disable the whole East Coast. It was a full-scale invasion by every major superpower in the world! They all united on behalf of the Aswanni people. They studied the scrolls and knew it was their duty to assist in the fulfillment of prophecy.

The Sacred Commander had gone across the world forming alliances preparing for that moment had America refused to pay reparations to the descendants of slaves.

He told me, "It was my last resort but it had to be done. I love America but certain powerful entities within the U.S. government and military wouldn't have paid the tab without a war."

He had also strategically taken those lawmakers hostage who opposed any real progression of Blacks in America. Those covert racists who had the power to decide the fate of millions of Blacks at the stroke of a pen. An ultimatum was given. Pay that tab or risk creating World War III.

Aftermath (75)

Many moons after the "American Civil Race War" King Aswad appeared to the Sacred Commander and me, while we were walking through a small village near the new capital of Aswanna once construction was complete. King Aswad was commenting on topics concerning the future of Aswanna and Africa when I asked Aswad,

"Why did prophecy have to be fulfilled in this era?"
I mean, why not any other time period in human history?"

Aswad answered, "Had you both not aligned yourselves with prophecy and broken the spell our people were under; they would have been a permanently subjugated people entangled in an elaborate illusionary Jim Crow caste system."

"That's social engineering at its finest," the Commander interjected."I just couldn't have allowed that to happen at the dawn of the millennium."

That just led to another question. "Besides prophecy, what would make every major superpower in the world want to ride with us? And actually invade the United States?!"

The Fountain (76)

The Sacred Commander had a small and disabled elderly man with him. I learned he was the elderly lady's husband whom Benjamin Sutton introduced me to at his home those years ago. He labored along with us and the soldiers as we trekked our way through the lush and beautiful rainforest in Aswanna. The Commander and I were making small conservation when we reached a lake and waterfall. "Look," the Commander pointed to the lake. "Nation, all I need you to do is get into the water."

"Alright, whatever," I answered, somewhat puzzled by the Commander's request. I took my clothes off

240

down to my boxers and dove into the lake. I swam around for a moment then asked, "Now what?"

The Commander replied, "Now watch this." He motioned for the disabled old fellow to get into the lake. The Aswanni monks who were also there helped him. When he got in waist-deep, the monks dipped him into the water, resembling a baptism. Afterwards, he arose from the baptism and approached the bank of the lake. Astonishingly, his features began to change and his skin regenerated, he seemed to be getting younger! We all gasped in amazement! When he reached the bank of the lake, he started "pop-locking" and jumping with joy!

The Commander explained to me what happened. "The reason the world powers rode with us is because they had analyzed the scrolls. When you resurrected the castle along with the Earth stopping its rotation, the day I was born that made them take those manuscripts seriously.

Those manuscripts also stated that the so-called mythical fountain of youth, which is proven true, would be found here somewhere in Africa during the eve of the Millennia. Only those who were pure-hearted and ascended to the highest levels of the ancient order of Apex Omegas would know that it would be located here in Aswanna.

Coronation / Celebration Intergalactic Contact (77)

Another full moon or two after the trip to the fountain of youth there was a Global Celebration and Coronation. The twelve-day celebration was in honor of defeating that deep dark element that shadowed the United States Government. The secret cabal had known that the keepers of the fountains activating power would be born in the U.S. They'd also known that had the keeper survived, he'd live for hundreds of years and be able to bring balance to the world before transitioning into eternity.

The coronation was created to inaugurate "The New World Supreme Steward." The whole world watched as I humbly accepted the two African star diamonds. Yeah, those two huge diamonds that England's royal family had in their possession. One was mounted on the crown, the other the staff. One of the diamonds was remounted on a platinum and gold crown to fit my head. Those diamonds were returned to Africa as a diplomatic sign of reverence.

As I was about to be crowned, we were all stunned by the spectacle that occurred in the sky. Twenty-one unidentified objects formed a twelve-pointed Omega Guard star! As I watched along with others in utter amazement, the Commander explained what was happening.

"The Pri-mega-nie," the ones that our ancestors labeled as Gods, were the beings who gave them the elixir, which was the essence of the fountain, those thousands of years ago! They are acknowledging their satisfaction and are endorsing you as The New World Supreme Steward!"

"The Pri-mega-nie" are an elite species of beings who are judges. They are a part of the intergalactic federation from the Andromeda galaxy. For eons, their sole purpose has been to go throughout the universe creating balance amongst species of evolved beings. On Earth, the threat of annihilation to humanity propelled the Pri-mega-nie, not only to endorse their approval of the New World Supreme Steward but to also protect him while he completes his mission.

7-day Theory (78)

For all you readers out there who want to know who the Sacred Commander and his aunt were, I'm going to let you all figure that out yourselves. He is now emeritus to the throne. Yeah, shit we came a long way from being street niggas, lost in the belly of America, to being leaders of our own country! The journey up to this point has been completely unbelievable! I have to pinch myself sometimes to make sure this is all real! I would never have thought in my wildest dreams, I'd become some global entity that would be influencing and guiding generations to come. I'm truly humbled every time it crosses my mind. This is where I sign off! I am Nation Omega Lord and these are the memoirs of the Prophet Street Poet…

Peace, Power, and Prosperity…

Essay

Although this body of work is pure fiction, this Black utopian urban fantasy novel was written to hopefully paint a picture that creates an "Elevated" narrative for future generations.

While writing this novel, I daydreamed of helping to bridge the gap between ages, institutions and subcultures within Black America.

There is so much that could be written concerning the upliftment and advancement of our people. I will keep this essay brief but as profound as I can. If you are at odds with what I've written after reading this, just understand that these are just my thoughts and theories after studying the condition of our people since the "Emancipation Proclamation."

Our inheritance is what has been withheld from us. Our ancestors, who toiled the soil of this land from sun up to sun down for centuries, made America one of the most prosperous nations ever to exist. Yet the slaves who were freed during Emancipation never received compensation. Just momentarily put yourself in our ancestors' shoes; we're distraught after working for 40 hrs that week and being denied a check. Just imagine that happening for a lifetime!

Our ancestors didn't arrive here on their own as immigrants; they were brought here in bondage. They were denied fundamental liberties of generating income that could produce generational wealth. That narrative has continued to persist over time. So, to this very day building generational wealth has been virtually an enigma for most of us. Just surviving has been our primary goal. The intricate and often unseen hand, through the uneven application of laws, has notoriously stifled any real progress for decades.

Remember this: the flow of information will be vital to our survival towards the rise of ascendancy as a people. For instance, the word reparation. While incarcerated, I conducted a study to see who would know what the word means. Out of 50 people, only 14 knew what it meant and how it applies to our people.

I also read an article in the Forward Times by Dr. Julianne Malveaux, an economist, author and Dean of the College of Ethnic Studies at Cal State LA. The article's topic was "Please Run For the School Board." In the article, she pleads for progressive Blacks to run for school board. She pleads for the obvious because of the flow of information and the indoctrination of misinformation being streamlined to our children. You have legislators and politicians who seek to continue the whitewashing of our young people's minds by injecting their ideology in our schools. And they're doing this by using low-turn-out, low-budget races to grab power," states Dr. Malveaux.

No outsider should be able to water down, distract us or downplay our history and struggle. We are a strong, powerful, and persevering people. Don't get distracted by this illusionary spell of equality. The fact remains that although we are a minority, we're the majority in every category detrimental to our existence.

Being stalled out of our inheritance is one of the main reasons. Right now, that tab is in the trillions! And as I type this over 40 million descendants of those who held slaves and 240 plus companies still benefit from the revenue made from the backs of our ancestors' labor. That money didn't just disappear!

You must advocate for your inheritance if you value your children, communities and people! Nowadays, we need more than one stream of income just to live above the poverty line. So many of us turn to the "streets" to supplement what is needed to sustain our lives. An extra half a mill, a change that right!

If we don't fight on behalf of the legacy of our ancestors and future generations that come after us, then how will history view this generation? Like the great Black Panther, Bobby Seale did in their era...Seize the Time!

I'm signing off with my universal greeting and closing, which is......

Peace, Power and Prosperity...

I must continuously challenge myself because it gives me a sense of purpose. I have yet to reach my peak and I may never do, but the challenge in life, as far as my life goes, is to try...

D. Jones

"Until the Lion learns how to write, every story will glorify the hunter"…
–African proverb..

"Finally, confident in my own skin,
Go on this journey with me; you gone win,
It takes time to climb to higher echelons,
To be the leader, in this hip hop pantheon…"

Bars from the song:
"Black Butterfly Juggernaut"

First off, this is a special notation in remembrance of my family members that transitioned to eternity, since I've been released. Francis Carson, Christopher "Chris Cross" Murray, and the dude who raised me, my stepfather Mr. Wilbert Clark...Those attributes that I've acquired from each of you, I hold dear and utilize daily.

Shout out to the ones who stood with me during my time of reflection......
To my lil sister, who is the real strength of the family...
Like that Jeezy song "What I gotta do"...
Anything you ever need, I'm always there...
To my babe bro, keep on pushing, you on your shit right now nigga!

Remember what we talked about, doing it for Mama!

To my street sister Memory. It's been 25-plus years, baby! We may fade out for a while, but we always find our way back to each other. I am amazed by how much you have accomplished in such little time! You're truly an inspiration.

A big shout out to my nigga, "Ace SouthWest Red Line Boogie!" We've been through the trenches and back; you know it's till death do us part!

What's up Jykeese!! Yea bitch we on our way! Love you my nigga!

To Cookie….
I would have never heard the end of it, had I not given you a shout-out! You know what it is…

Special thanks to Ms. Carter…

And last but not least is my brother from another mother, Jay Essence. Ever since we were young running through them Southwest streets, you believed in a nigga, even when I didn't believe in myself.

This one last big shout is for the countless others who took the time to extend their hand and reach out in any form. I appreciated that. Sometimes, a kind word is all a leader needs to succeed.

Hey...Now breathe baby, you've just been born...

QUIZ

1) Where did Tiara first meet Nation?

2) What was the history behind Nation's mother?

3) When did Jay first find out Nation had the gift of prophecy?

4) Did Nation ever claim "baby Nation" as his son?

5) What happened the day the Sacred Commander was born?

6) Who was taking pictures of Nation in L.A. while he was at the gas station?

7) Who would the Sacred Commander and his Aunt be in real life?

8) What did Aswad tell Harmony about her history?

9) How did Harmony know how Nation felt when his senses were elevated?

10) Who tried to assassinate Nation?

Answers

1. Cinnamon Lane

2. Ebony Lord was a black panther who was acquitted of kidnapping and murder. She was accused of murdering a judge.

3. During the interview at the Breakfast Club.

4. Yes. God son.

5. The Earth Stood Still

6. The FBI agents

7. Tupac and Assata Shakur

8. In Harmony's past, she was an Aswanni diplomat.

9. She was able to feel what he felt.

10. Rebel carried out the assassination.

Nation's sanity is tested when the spirit of his ancestor, King Aswad periodically visits him, claiming to seek Nation's assistance in fulfilling an age-old prophecy. He also appears to Nation's mother, who is serving time in prison along with his lioness Harmony, who verifies his existence.

Now, the trillion-dollar question is: Can Nation escape the pitfalls and traps that have been systemically set decades in advance?

Go on a journey of epic proportions as Nation guides you through his spiritual, political & cultural metamorphosis, all while dodging a government conspiracy to assassinate him, to become the most influential Hip Hop artist of all time......

THE PROPHET STREET POET

Made in the USA
Monee, IL
17 October 2024